Quentin climbed over a sofa to reach her. His mouth turned dry at the splintered six-by-six floor joist inches from her head. Chips of wood dotted her fallen body.

Her chest rose and fell in small increments, easing the tightness in his ribs.

He smoothed the silky hair back from her pale face. "Emma? Wake up."

Her eyelashes fluttered, setting off butterflies in his stomach. His fingers trailed down the side of her face. He leaned in close.

The delightful aroma of wildflowers assailed him, blinding him to everything but the universe of Emma. She had to be all right. He willed her eyes to open again.

She blinked, and relief swept through him. He touched his lips to hers. "Emma?"

Praise for Seeing Red

"Set in modern day, suburban Maryland, Ms. Toussaint's character descriptions leave you wanting to know more about Emma and Quentin's delightful family members. Her suspenseful dialogue and plots have you rooting for our hero and heroine from the very beginning. This is a great story that you won't want to put down, and I would recommend it to anyone wanting a sweet, non-graphic romance." –*Long and Short Reviews*

"Read *Seeing Red*. It's witty, fun, and fast-paced. One of the better romances I've read in months! I give it five flutes of champagne." –*Cocktail Reviews*

"An excellent read." –*Night Owl Romance*

This title is also available as an eBook.

Seeing Red

Maggie Toussaint

Cover Art by *Laura Shinn*

Muddle House Publishing
PO Box 2119
Darien, GA 31305

Publishing History
Digital book, Freya's Bower, 2007
Second ed. digital and trade paperback, Muddle House, 2011
Print ISBN-13: 978-0-9833614-1-1

Published in the United States of America

DEDICATION

This book is dedicated to my sisters who put up with a lot and my husband who puts up with even more. Thank you for being part of my life and listening to my crazy ideas.

ACKNOWLEDGMENTS

This book first debuted in the Country Roads critique group. Members Barbara Cummings, Gail Barrett, Susan Dudics Dean, and Rebecca McTavish were instrumental in shaping the story and encouraging me to continue to write in the face of rejection. MK Trent, my longtime friend and beta-reader, also provided valuable input. I'd also like to acknowledge editor Faith Bicknell Brown of Freya's Bower who saw a spark in this story and helped polish it to publication standards.

CHAPTER ONE

So close.

She'd been so close to starting her life over.

Why'd that banker need three signatures for the loan?

Why didn't her sisters sign the paperwork?

She wasn't irresponsible.

Emma slopped more paint on the old barn. Life wasn't fair. She'd taken care of everyone else—why couldn't it be her turn now?

Tears threatened. She blinked them away. She'd cried her share of tears already. She might be down, but she wasn't done.

Quitting wasn't her way. She'd figure this out, even if she had to do the work by herself.

Paint streamed off the end of her paintbrush. Thin scarlet beads trickled down the splintery boards and pooled in the late-summer grass. She slapped another brush full of color on the barn. Speckles of paint dotted her bare feet.

Time to shake off the chains of the past.

Her dead-end job.

Her ex-boyfriend boss.

The loud thumping of her heart blotted out the happy twitter of nearby birds. Paint fumes filled her head, dulling her senses. Her field of vision narrowed to the crimson paint staining the old barn.

Dreams.

What a waste of time.

Heartlys ended up with shattered dreams.

Emma swallowed the lump in her throat. She'd find a way out of this mess. She'd been in worse situations and found success. Comforted by that assurance, she swabbed on her last bit of paint.

Out of the blue, her skin prickled. Something registered in her peripheral vision. Something shiny.

Shoes.

"Aah!" She whirled. In what seemed like freeze-frame action, an arc of red paint flew from her brush. It splattered across the crisp white fabric of the man's shirt and his striped navy tie.

Good grief.

She'd ruined his clothes. What a terrible time to be a klutz, when she needed every cent she could scrape together. No telling what men's clothing cost.

Aghast, she stared at the man. If she overlooked the red paint on his attire, he looked like he'd stepped off the pages of a glossy magazine advertisement.

All right, Mr. Tall, Dark, and Gorgeous, what wrong turn brought you here?

Her hand covered her chest. "Omigosh! You startled me. I'm sorry about slopping paint on your clothes."

He dismissed his clothing with a glance. "A little paint never hurt anything."

She had to do something to fix it, but what? Maybe she could blot the worst of it off. She dropped her wet brush, tugged the bandana off her head, and started toward him. "But your shirt. That tie. I've ruined them."

His open palm blocked her momentum. "It's okay, truly, it is. I shouldn't have given you such a start. I apologize for not announcing I was here."

His voice sent a ripple of awareness through her. Dark brown eyes swept her from head to toe. The corners of his mouth edged up. Emma's pulse skittered. She inventoried his physical features. Six feet tall. Wavy brown hair. Angular face. Broad shoulders. Trim hips. Long legs.

Her face warmed with approval. Darn. She'd always had a thing for long-legged men. Not that it mattered what she liked. She'd misjudged another male recently. She wouldn't repeat that mistake again.

Oh, Lord.

Her clothes.

This halter-top was a bit revealing, and she'd been meaning to lose five pounds. She sucked in her tummy and hoped to brazen it out. A gust of wind grazed her skin, breezing through the hole in the seat of her faded jean shorts. She'd worn sunshine-yellow undies today in hopes of brightening her mood.

Heat flooded up her neck.

Her fingers spasmed on the thin cotton bandana. She had to say something quick. "Don't apologize. I get tunnel vision when I'm working. I should've paid closer attention. I feel awful for ruining your clothes. Please let me buy you a new shirt and tie."

He shrugged. "There's no need. I should have said something sooner, but I didn't want to interrupt your painting. I'm looking for Emma Heartly."

Her mouth dropped open. This gorgeous man came to see her? Did she win the male supermodel lottery or something? Be still my heart.

She fanned herself. "You found her. How may I help you?"

"I'm Quentin Stone. Of Stone Construction." He handed her his business card. "You scheduled an estimate on a home improvement project for today."

At the casual brush of his fingers in her palm, the air around her sparkled with energy. The charged current scattered her wits. She fumbled the card into her pocket along with her bandana. She shot him a covert glance but he appeared to be unaffected by the casual touch.

Puzzling.

The scientist in her wanted to repeat the experiment to verify the unusual result. The entrepreneur in her wanted to bottle his blatant sex appeal. She could make a fortune. The Heartly in her knew she'd do neither. "So I did."

"Pleased to meet you," he said.

His deep voice rumbled through her, sending a shiver down her spine. She bit her lip to clear her senses. So what if it made her knees weak to look at him? Heartlys had rotten luck with handsome men.

She straightened. "I'm sorry you've come all this way. My financing fell through yesterday afternoon, and in my disappointment I forgot to cancel our appointment."

Confusion temporarily clouded his appealing face. "Since I'm here, why not take advantage of the free estimate we offer? Stone Construction has sixty years of expertise in building and renovating houses."

His marketing pitch surprised her. Nevertheless, she couldn't afford him on her salary. Her cheek twitched. "No thanks."

"I might be able to suggest inexpensive solutions you haven't previously considered."

He'd wasted his time driving out here from Baltimore. She couldn't impose on him any further. "I'd be taking advantage of you."

"You aren't taking advantage if I offer you a free service," he said. "Let's take a look-see. It'd save me a trip later should you change your mind."

The friendly glint in his brown eyes weakened her resolve.

She frowned. Everyone knew you didn't get something for nothing. She'd feel obligated to hire him if he toured her ramshackle house. She glanced at him. Eagerness brightened his magnetic features. Interesting. He really wanted to see the house.

What would it hurt to humor him?

She could be level-headed and refuse, or she could live the dream of rehabbing the house. She'd done the cautious approach her entire life and gotten nowhere.

Time for a change-up.

"Okay. I'll pump you for ideas. Then I'll send you on your way without the promise of any work. That will make you happy, right?"

Smile lines wreathed his eyes. "Right."

Her heart lightened. She gestured towards the house with her paint-speckled hand. "Follow me. I'll show you my broken dinosaur. You can tell me how to glue it back together."

He matched her stride as they walked up the slight hill. This handsome stranger with the inherent authority of an archangel intrigued her. Athletic-looking men like Quentin didn't exist in her world at Orbital Scientific. He looked like he could bench press her car without breaking a sweat.

He could talk two-by-fours and I-beams all he wanted, she decided. The longer she indulged in her rehab fantasy, the better. With that thought, a burden lifted from her shoulders.

She was living the dream.

The sky above seemed bluer, the white clouds fluffier. Even the birds chirped louder. Beneath her bare feet, the lush grass cushioned her stride. All was well in suburban Maryland.

A yellow tabby cat darted ahead of her. A trail of mewing kittens scampered close behind, determined to keep up.

Had the silence stretched too long? She didn't want him to feel unwelcome. Better say something.

She waved at the feline parade. "That's Zelda and her brood. She hopes I'll feed her every time I enter the house. It's a regular production each time I open the door. Do you need a cat? I can't keep them all."

He shot her a sidelong look of horror. "No, I don't need a cat."

Heat rose to her face. Good Lord. Why did she mention the cats? Men avoided cat ladies. If she wanted to hear his lovely, free ideas, she'd better talk about something else.

But what?

This wasn't a social call, though she might enjoy that fantasy as well. Ever since she'd taken his business card, she'd been rattled. Living a dream was harder than she thought. There were no standard operating procedures to follow. She'd have to wing it.

Climbing the creaking porch steps, she marshaled her thoughts into order. The worn indentations in the wooden risers reminded her of her heritage. "My great grandfather built this house eighty years ago. My idea is to turn this place into a bed and breakfast. As you can see, the exterior needs work."

She pointed to the tall, narrow windows on the weathered wood siding. "The missing shutters are in the barn. A storm damaged them a few years ago. One of the window panes needs to be replaced."

His pencil scribbled noisily on his clipboard. Emma had an overpowering urge to see what he'd written. She half-wished his notes were personal in nature. Something along the lines of "Great Legs" or "Nice Smile." Not that she would have a real chance with a hunk like Quentin Stone. Worldly men like him didn't shop for thirty-year-old brides.

She stopped to pet her slumbering hound sprawled on the porch. "Agnes doesn't move very fast these days."

Quentin nodded towards the dog. "I noticed."

She glanced sharply at him. "Oh? Did she bark at you earlier?"

He shrugged. "Not that I could tell."

A wave of relief swept through her. If Agnes couldn't be bothered about Quentin Stone, then she wouldn't be worried either. Agnes had never been wrong about people before. The dog had growled at Joel Frazier—too bad she hadn't taken the dog-o-meter warning to heart when it came to him.

She entered the house, and her nose wrinkled at the

musty smell. "Watch your step. The floor boards near the window need to be replaced." She nodded toward the plywood-patched window. "Water damage from that storm."

The water-blackened floorboards in the front parlor looked awful. Did he think she was accustomed to living in squalor? Her fingernails bit into her palms. She tamped down her anxiety. It had no place in her dream. Besides, his perception of her lifestyle didn't matter.

"Let's start at the top." Emma led him up to the second floor. "There are five bedrooms up here." She gestured toward the rooms in a game show hostess fashion, glad she'd tidied up her bedroom this morning. "Though I'd like to add a bathroom to each bedroom, I'm not sure if there is enough space."

He examined each room in turn, his hand gliding reverently over the chipped beadboard. "Three of these rooms are large enough to modify. These deep closets will make a good start on your new bathrooms. The smaller rooms might share the existing bathroom."

"Oh." Her mood tanked and peaked as she considered the ramifications. "Only put in three bathrooms? That would save money, but it wouldn't be as convenient for some guests."

He observed the vintage lighting fixtures. "You'll need an electrician to bring your wiring up to code."

An electrician? She hadn't considered the ancient wiring. "Good point."

"You'll also need a plumber to install and upgrade the bathroom fixtures. How old is the septic system?"

She swallowed around the lump in her throat. Oh, dear. Rehab involved much more than pounding a few nails or adding a layer of paint. "I have no idea."

His level gaze held her spellbound. "My guess is that you'll need to put in a new system. Since that involves digging up the yard, I recommend doing that soon to allow the grass time to establish a good root base."

He examined the rusty radiators, his long supple fingers skimming over the pipes. "You'll want to upgrade to central heat and air. You'll save time and money upgrading during your rehab."

"Great." Emma snapped out of her dreamworld. His suggestions cost serious money, way more than she planned to spend. Glumly, she directed him down the stairs. The dining room's brown walls depressed her. "This room is too dark. Wallpaper would add some cheer."

Quentin's eyes warmed as he touched the wood. "They don't make walnut paneling like this anymore. Be a shame to cover this up with wallpaper. You need a light colored wash to brighten the finish."

"Paint the paneling?"

"Not exactly. You'd have to strip off the existing finish. That gets pricey because of the labor involved, but it might be a place for you to start if you have the time to spare."

She brightened at the magic word of labor. Any handiwork she did would save her money. "Thanks for the tip." She envisioned her inn clientele eating a sumptious breakfast in the newly whitewashed dining room. This could work out.

"Give me a ballpark figure," she said. "How much would these repairs set me back?"

"I don't normally provide estimates without obtaining quotes from our subcontractors," Quentin hedged.

Emma needed to know a number. Dreaming about renovations made her bed and breakfast dream seem attainable. Having a number would help her plan out the phases of the project. "Surely you know what a job this size will cost."

"I shouldn't say without totaling each line item."

"Humor me," she insisted.

"I wouldn't want to give you the wrong impression about Stone Construction. We are a reputable company. We pride ourselves on the quality of our service."

Why was he being difficult? She needed to know a number for heaven's sake. How difficult could that be for a renovation expert? "Come on. You must have an idea. What am I looking at here? Twenty to thirty thousand?"

He exhaled slowly. "More like eighty."

His estimate knocked the wind out of her. "Eighty," she repeated dully. By her own accounting of what she would be saving in rent money since she'd moved out here, it would take her over eight years to accumulate eighty thousand dollars.

She couldn't work for Joel eight more years. It wasn't going to happen. Her best bet would be to convince her sisters to sign the papers for a mortgage. Right. When pigs could fly.

Her shoulders slumped in defeat. She turned towards the arched doorway. "The kitchen is through here. I want to replace the appliances but—"

A whiff of burning food assaulted her nostrils. "Not again!" Emma dashed into the kitchen for her brand new fire extinguisher.

She opened the ancient oven. A suffocating cloud of acrid smoke billowed toward her. "Oh, no."

Before she had time to act, Quentin's muscular

forearms closed around her. He lifted her out of harm's way and grabbed the fire extinguisher from the counter. White foam shot from the black barrel onto the smoking pan. She peered around his broad shoulders at the foul-smelling mess, heart in her throat.

She cursed under her breath, wishing this perfect man hadn't witnessed her latest cooking failure. She'd burned up another pan. Why couldn't she cook one blasted thing without ruining it?

The tension inside her demanded a release. With that, she threw open the sink window and hurled the pan into the back yard. It landed with a metallic clang amongst her collection of burnt pans.

"You'll need a new fire extinguisher," he observed.

"Believe me, I know the drill." She stomped away from the window, frustration churning in her gut.

He bent over the open oven door and prodded the heating element with his pencil. "I don't think there's any permanent damage."

"Lucky me." Despite her mood, she got a little thrill watching him, as her fantasy expanded to include him as her permanent handyman. She admired the way his jeans stretched across his hips. Yes, he would be very easy on the eyes.

He glanced over his shoulder at her. "Have you checked the temperature adjustment?"

Drat. He'd caught her looking. She swallowed her mortification to focus on the real problem. Why hadn't she thought to check the oven's calibration? The reaction temperature would've been the first thing she would have verified in a laboratory experiment. "I'll check into it."

He set down the fire extinguisher with a loud clank and glanced out her window. "How many times has this happened?"

Suddenly, it was all too much. She couldn't catch a break from her sisters, the bank or the oven. "How many days have I been here?"

He stared at her in silence.

Feeling remorse for her snarky tone, she blurted out the truth. "Seven times."

His mouth dropped open.

Her jaw clamped shut. She'd stunned him. So much for her impossible dreams of hiring him. He'd run out of here any minute now, glad to leave crazyville before it sucked him into the mire. If they crossed paths again, he'd remember she was a disaster. Between the kitchen fire and his ruined clothing, she'd made a lasting bad impression. "Cooking isn't my strong suit."

His continued silence rattled her, and she hastened to explain. "I haven't had much practice with cooking, but I have to learn how so that I can feed my future guests. People cook everyday. Experience will fix my problem."

His mouth finally closed. "Look, this is none of my business, but you shouldn't push your luck any farther. Do you have someone who can teach you to cook?"

Her chin rose at the implied insult. "I am a grown up. I know how to read. I'm teaching myself to cook."

"There's more to cooking than reading."

His dismissive words irked her. She'd had it with things going wrong.

Her job sucked. Her boyfriend betrayed her. Her sisters blocked the loan. The ruined pan paled in comparison. "This is none of your business."

"I see."

Anger sharpened her voice. "We're done here."

He raised his hands up in surrender. "I'm not telling

you anything you shouldn't already know. Don't shoot the messenger."

Emma rubbed her temples. Some of her tension eased, leaving confusion in its place. She shouldn't take out her frustration on a stranger. "I'm not blaming anyone. I have lots to do to get this place whipped into a bed and breakfast."

"Thanks for the tour. This is some house." Quentin held the door open for her. His pleasing woodsy fragrance wafted around her, creating a flutter in her heart again. "You'll do the renovations yourself?"

She didn't care for the note of disbelief in his voice. She knew which end of a hammer to use even if she couldn't cook. "Yes." She infused her words with an icy calm.

"Be careful. Construction is harder than cooking."

God save her from know-it-all-men. Especially good-looking ones. With her arms folded across her chest, she trailed him to his black Jeep. "Thank you, Mr. Expert."

He slammed the door of his Jeep shut. "I don't like sarcastic women."

"I don't like nosy contractors."

To Emma's dismay, he sat there, fingers frozen on the steering wheel. Had she stunned him with her witty repartee? Why didn't he leave? His head slowly turned to face her, and his long eyelashes swept her length. A flash of heat followed his lingering perusal. Excitement sizzled through her veins.

His gaze returned to her face. She drew in quick, shallow breaths. Why didn't he say something? Suddenly she realized his lips had finished moving. She had no idea what he'd said. How humiliating. "What?"

Maggie Toussaint

"Don't cook again until you get another fire extinguisher."

She'd hoped his parting words would be poignant or meaningful, something she could dine on for years to come. Instead, he'd told her what to do.

Like Joel.

Emma frowned. "I don't like bossy men."

His dark eyes narrowed, compacting his unsettling gaze. "Who does?"

With that, he executed a tight three-point turn. She fingered his business card in her pocket. First thing Monday morning she'd mail his office a check for his ruined clothing. That would be the end of Quentin Stone's disturbing presence in her life.

Her friend Lucy would enjoy hearing about this little adventure. As Emma considered what to tell her work friend, a small white car barreled up the narrow driveway. The large dust plume behind the car indicated its rapid speed.

Oh, no.

Unless someone yielded, the white sedan would crash into Quentin's Jeep.

CHAPTER TWO

At the last minute, the black Jeep veered onto the grassy shoulder. Emma sighed in relief. Good thing Quentin had sense enough to avoid a collision. Her sister Maddy, the driver of the white sedan, drove like a little Jack Russell dog, charged with attitude.

Maddy's horn blared. Emma's stomach knotted at the sudden blast. Her sister expected her to forget about the rehab. In the past, Emma had allowed Maddy to prevail because the end result hadn't mattered to her. Not this time. The Heartly Inn mattered to Emma, very much so. It was her dream, her escape from drudgery.

Apparently her sister's scathing phone conversation last night hadn't been the final word on the mortgage subject. She shuddered. Neither of them would change their minds, so why continue to debate property ownership? It distressed her to be the cause of so much family friction, but it couldn't be helped.

Emma scooped up a sun-warmed kitten from the ground. If push came to shove, she could use its sharp claws for self-defense.

Her sister shot out of the car like a rocket, her chic black jumpsuit out of place in this time-worn setting. "Who was that?"

She reeled at the razor sharp edge of Maddy's voice. "No one."

"Hi, Emma." Her younger sister's voice brimmed with cheerfulness. White daisies splashed the top of Beverly's denim sundress. "The logo on the Jeep said Stone Construction."

"Stone Construction?" Maddy smacked her palm on the hood of her car. "You can't get a loan for this place without our permission. We all own equal shares of the farm."

Emma stroked the kitten's head five times before she replied. "I know that."

"So what was he doing here?"

"I invited him. Don't worry about it."

"What are you up to, Emma? We didn't agree to give you the property. Tell me the real reason he was here. What does he want?"

He wanted her house. He wanted her, too, judging by the heated glance he'd turned her way. Flattering but utterly impossible. She had her eye on a different goal. Launching her new business would require her total concentration. She didn't have time for a relationship now.

She didn't have time for bossy sisters either. She'd sacrificed for them, but now she could do something for herself. Something that didn't involve catering to Maddy's volatile temper.

She held Maddy's gaze. "I don't have to tell you a blasted thing, Madeline."

16

Beverly stepped in front of Maddy. "Em, she didn't mean to upset you. We're worried about you."

She arched an eyebrow at the good-sister-bad-sister routine. "Did you bring the signed Quit Claim Deed?"

"No." Maddy's turquoise eyes flashed in anger. "We won't sign it."

Emma turned towards the door. "Then there's no point in having this conversation."

"Be reasonable. You can't expect us to sign away our inheritance." Beverly stroked the cat. "Can I hold the kitty?"

Figured. Her baby sister wanted her only source of solace. She handed Beverly the kitten and thrust her hands into her pockets. "I'm not asking you to give anything away. The Quit Claim Deed is temporary."

"So you say," Maddy sneered. "What if you sell off the property the moment our backs are turned?"

Emma's wafer-thin hold on her patience snapped. She spun on her heel to face the most lethal of the sisterly tag team. "Haven't I always done what's best for the family? Didn't I allow each of you to follow your own dream?"

A dark red stain marred Maddy's features. "So what? That has nothing to do with this."

She unclenched her jaw. "It says everything about who I am."

"Big deal." Maddy gestured wildly. "You've bossed us around for years. The farm is our home. I don't want strangers staying here."

Emma took deep breaths to slow her pounding heart. While it felt good to vent her frustrations, she didn't want to cause a permanent rift in the family. "Have you ever stayed at a bed and breakfast? Everyone there is very friendly."

"You've always been a scientist." Beverly's voice quivered.

Tears welled in her eyes. Her sisters didn't know her at all. "Grandma convinced me science would pay well. She was right, but I don't like science. I've never liked it."

"What?"

The collective uproar knocked the starch out of Emma. She'd always been strong for her family, but she couldn't continue to put them first. She stumbled up the porch steps to sit beside her dog. Both sisters followed, both talking a mile a minute.

She hated strong emotions, hated herself for causing this conflict, but, most of all, she hated people hovering over her. She wasn't backing down on this, but she'd let them stew a few minutes until they got used to the idea. Then she'd set them straight.

"I have rights to this property," Maddy said. "I won't sign them away."

Her wait-and-see strategy vanished. "I'm not asking you to relinquish your rights forever. Only long enough for me to get a short-term loan. Then I'll deed your shares back."

"This is my inheritance. It's all I have left of Mama's family," Maddy asserted.

"Don't you think I know that?" Her stomach knotted at Maddy's stubbornness. She glanced over at her baby sister. "Beverly?"

Beverly's chin jutted out. "I won't sign either."

Though their solidarity caused her heart to sink, Emma couldn't quit now. "I need your help on this. Without a clear title to the property, I can't borrow money for the renovations. This is my dream. Running a bed and breakfast is what I want to do."

"I can't sign that paper. You're asking too much of me." Maddy clomped down the steps in a huff.

The dog bounded after her sister around the side of the house. "Traitor," Emma mumbled under her breath. With defiance, she met her baby sister's gaze.

Beverly wore an odd expression. "All these years. Why didn't you say anything about not liking science before now?"

She'd done what she had to do, but she couldn't do it anymore. "I didn't realize how miserable I was until recently. I've always had this bed and breakfast idea in the back of my mind. It isn't a spur of the moment decision."

"What would Grandma say? I bet she's spinning in her grave at the thought of you quitting that job." Beverly released the kitten and leaned against the weathered porch railing.

No fair using Grandma to make her feel guilty. She'd given up her childhood to provide for her family. She didn't owe them anything else. "It's time I did something for myself."

"But Emma, washing dishes is the only housework you're good at. Have you forgotten you can't cook?"

The corners of Emma's lips inched upward. "Kind of hard to forget my culinary disasters, but I'm working on the problem. By the time I get this place fixed up, I'll be a gourmet chef."

"I don't know about that." Skepticism flickered across Beverly's face. "I love you, but you are a terrible cook."

"I'll get the hang of it." Emma's voice came out

sharper than she intended, and Beverly flinched. "I'm sorry, Sis. I didn't mean to yell at you."

"But there's no heat in this house. What will you do in the winter?"

"I'm hoping my sisters come to their senses before then."

Maddy strolled around the house carrying one of her burnt pans. "I see you've taken well-done to a whole new level. Even the critters won't eat this stuff."

She snatched the pan from her sister's hand. "Mistakes happen. I found out the oven is out of calibration."

"No kidding. We've known that for years."

"I didn't know."

"You'd have known if you spent more time here," Maddy said.

Her temper flared again. "I wasn't here because I had to work so that we could stay together. Did you forget what it's like to be dirt poor?"

Maddy stomped her booted foot. "No. And I'll never be that poor again. Which is why I can't sign that paper allowing you to go into debt."

While she stared at her paint-speckled hands, Emma marshaled a new argument. "Life is about change. You can't expect things to stay the same forever. If someone doesn't do something about this house, it won't be here much longer."

"Maybe I want it to fall down. Did you even think to ask what I wanted, Emma?"

She blinked. "I didn't think it mattered to you. You've repeatedly said you'd never live here again." She turned to her baby sister. "What about you?"

Beverly shifted from foot to foot. "I'm not sure what

I want. This is all so sudden."

Her admission jarred Emma into reflection. Was she being reckless? Was that why they were at an impasse? "I'm sorry. I'm not used to sharing responsibility with you two."

"We know." Maddy stared out over the meadow.

A heavy silence settled on the porch. The weight of her sisters' disapproval bowed Emma's shoulders. Why didn't they understand about her quest for happiness?

Beverly leaned forward to catch her eye. "How will you find a husband if you're stuck out here?"

"Finding a husband is a low priority for me." After Joel Frazier, she didn't care if she ever dated anyone again. He'd been her first foray back in the dating pool after a long dry spell. She'd thought she might be ready to settle down, but Joel wasn't the right man. His betrayal cut deep. Men were off her radar screen.

Except for a certain construction estimator. He'd held her attention.

"What about that good-looking guy you were seeing?" Beverly persisted.

Her fingers curled into a tight ball. "Dating Joel was the biggest mistake of my life."

Maddy turned back around. "How so?"

"He was everything Grandma warned us about." She grimaced. "Handsome, successful, and rotten to the core. I should have known better."

"But?"

She inhaled slowly to center herself. "Most of my classmates are married. I was afraid I had missed the boat. I knew better than to trust Joel, but I did it anyway. I learned from my mistake. The Heartly family motto is once again etched into my brain."

"Don't date handsome men," her sisters chimed in unison.

She nodded. "Yes. I'd quit my job in a heartbeat, but it pays well. Molecular biology jobs don't grow on trees. I have an eighty thousand dollar rehab job to finance. Besides, Orbital is the only scientific laboratory of its kind in town."

Beverly paled. "You'd go ahead with the rehab without a mortgage?"

She spoke from her heart. "Yep."

"You can't work all day, drive an hour to get home, and do repairs all night," Beverly sputtered. "It's ludicrous to consider it."

Emma glanced at the setting sun. Not much light left in the day. "What's ludicrous is me standing here arguing with you when I have so much to do."

"When's the last time you used a hammer?" Maddy asked. "You'll be knocking on my door before the end of the month."

She was all too aware of the obstacles in her way. The two biggest obstacles stood right in front of her. "Fat chance. I hate living in the city. I hate my job. And I hate my boss."

"Get another job," Maddy snapped. "Meet another guy. You're still young. You'd be attractive if you fixed yourself up a little."

"That's a low blow." Just because she didn't wear Maddy's body-hugging style of clothing didn't mean she didn't care about her appearance.

Beverly clapped her hands twice in rapid succession. "Girls, girls. Don't squabble."

"Yes, Grandma," they chorused at the familiar admonition.

"We probably all need therapy, but we've got to make the best of the situation," Beverly said. "So our family was a little dysfunctional. Isn't everyone's? I mean, what is normal?"

"Normal is having fun while you're young," Maddy said.

"Normal is following your own dream," Emma added.

"Normal is not squabbling with your only blood relatives," Beverly countered. "We're family. We should get along."

Emma returned Maddy's heated glare. "Sign that Quit Claim Deed."

"Get another job," Maddy countered.

"I don't want another science job." Emma's pulse thundered in her ears. She had to get through to them. "I want a new career. I want to be free of the past."

Hurt flashed through Maddy's eyes. "We're part of your past. Are you ditching us, too?"

Was she serious? "You're my sisters. We'll always be family. I'm proud of everything you've accomplished. Now it's my turn to reach for a dream. Running the Heartly Inn is mine."

Beverly's knuckles gleamed like pearls on the weathered railing. "So, you're stuck with us?"

A light went on in Emma's head. "You're afraid that I'm turning into Dad."

Maddy stared at her. "Mama thought he'd always be there for her."

The implied comparison launched Emma to her feet. "Our father was a jerk. He doesn't deserve a minute of your consideration."

Her sisters exchanged a knowing glance. "Yes, but

he went from being our dad to being gone forever in one day," Beverly blurted.

She swallowed hard. How could she convince them she'd always be dependable? "I'm not like him. I'm not going anywhere. This is our home. You're my family."

"Time will tell." Maddy tugged on Beverly's arm. "Let's go."

With relief, Emma watched them drive away. The bonds that held them together had stretched thin, but they hadn't broken. She still had a family.

She stared at the fire-hardened lump of bread in her hand. She couldn't change the past, but she wouldn't let it control her future either. Unless she got an advanced degree, she'd be trapped at Orbital. College wasn't great the first time around. Why would she do it again?

As Emma headed toward the shadowed kitchen, thoughts of her childhood pinged through her brain. Her father's abandonment. Her mother's fatal breast cancer. Her grandparents' poverty. She'd overcome those challenges...somehow.

She flipped on the kitchen light. Life was about choices. Grandma had drilled that fact into Emma's brain. She'd said Emma was smart enough to do anything she wanted. Emma had believed her.

Now Emma wanted a B&B. "So what if I don't know beans about plumbing or putting up walls? I'll figure it out," she murmured.

Pipes were like connectable toys. You pushed them together until they stuck. How difficult could it be to fix this place up? Men did it every day. Men with less education than she had.

The thought cheered her. She tossed the burnt loaf pan out the kitchen window again. She was smart. She would change her future.

* * *

With the prickly redhead from his last call still on his mind, Quentin missed the first turn off into his condo complex. He'd much admired Emma's womanly curves. Her bottom-line attitude also impressed him.

If ever a woman needed his help, she did. Her living room floor potentially had structural issues. That house needed more than a few coats of paint. He loved old places like that two-story Victorian.

He loved women, too.

But Emma Heartly wasn't for him. With one stepmother and his three stepsisters telling him what to do, he had enough outspoken females in his life already. He certainly didn't need another woman ordering him around.

He should stay far away from Emma.

Who was he kidding? Touching her had sparked a need deep within him to touch her again...and again. His blood hummed at the thought of the feminine challenge she presented. That passionate personality. Those inviting curves.

Not a good sign. He'd had these kinds of fixations before. In the past, he indulged his inclinations. He'd wound up with four different fiancées. He'd also had four broken engagements.

He turned into the second entrance of his housing complex and navigated through a series of turns to his place.

He should ignore his interest in Emma. At a minimum, that would save him the cost of another diamond ring. It would allow him to determine if his fascination for her stemmed from the adrenaline of putting out that fire in her kitchen or something more enduring.

His stepsister's car occupied his parking space, giving him something else to worry about. Why was Jeanie still here? Her house-cleaning business kept her employed, but it allowed him no privacy. He had to hide his cookbooks before she came to clean for him.

Men cooked in other families. Not his family.

If his father hadn't made such a big deal about real men not cooking, he wouldn't mind if the family knew about his pastime. According to Quentin Senior, Stones were manly men. They stayed out of the kitchen. Consequently, his passion for gourmet cooking was a private matter, a closely-held secret.

He stepped over her cleaning supplies stacked inside the doorway of his penthouse condominium. "Jeanie?"

"In here."

He followed her leaden voice. She sprawled on his leather sofa, flipping through a Road and Track magazine. A sudden chill shot down his spine. Had she discovered his secret?

He sat down on the black leather recliner across from her, not sure what to say next. He couldn't imagine why she'd waited for him. Normally, she zipped in and out during his workday. "Hey, Sis."

"Where ya been? I've been waiting for you."

"Working. Had an estimate out at the lake."

"Oh."

She flipped through several more pages. "What's wrong, Jeanie?"

"Do you think there's something wrong with us? Do

you think we aren't capable of commitment?"

He glanced at her left hand. The large diamond she habitually wore was absent. He exhaled his relief. His secret was safe. "I take it the wedding is off?"

"I never want to see Harrison again." She sniffed. "He's mean."

Harrison James loved Jeanie, had loved her since high school. "What happened?"

Her eyes glistened. "Harrison told me I had to drop my male clients. He said it isn't appropriate for me to be cleaning for other men."

He refrained from laughing aloud. Harrison trusted Jeanie with his heart, but he didn't trust other men to keep their hands to themselves. A smile touched the corner of his lips. "Is he planning on keeping you in a bubble for the next fifty years?"

"It's not funny." She threw the magazine on the coffee table. "He can't boss me around like that. I'd lose half of my business if I followed his orders."

Emma Heartly's face flashed through Quentin's thoughts again. He had no right to call her his, but the thought of her with another man bothered him. He understood Harrison's point of view. "He's trying to keep you safe. He doesn't want anything to happen to you."

"He isn't trying to ruin my life?"

He remembered the rightness of Emma's touch. They weren't dating, but he wanted to keep her away from other men. He wanted to see her by candlelight. To see if her eyes would glaze over with passion for him.

He couldn't blame Harrison for trying to keep Jeanie exclusively his. He'd do the same thing with Emma if he had half the chance. "Definitely not."

* * *

At the weekly Stone-Sterling family dinner, Quentin fixed his gaze on his stepmother's face. Dottie Sterling Stone savored her first bite of the crème brulée he'd made. Her bright candy-apple red scarf caught his eye. A red scarf was the first gift his father had ever given her. She never went without one now.

Her face wreathed in smiles. "Quentin, you have to tell us where you get these marvelous desserts. I want to buy stock in that restaurant."

He grimaced, hating that he had to keep this side of himself hidden from his family. "If I did that, then Sunday dinner wouldn't be special."

His brother John scraped his dish clean. "This custard goo is okay, but my favorite is that apple stuff. Bring that next week."

Tabby scowled at John. "Apple Pan Dowdy is yummy, but we'd have it every week if it was up to you."

His younger brother peered out of the bay window. Alf's grim expression matched his unrelieved black attire. "Jeanie, your fiancée is here."

She leapt to her feet. "Harrison is not my fiancée."

As one, the family chorused, "Right."

"You don't understand." Her gaze flitted toward the door. "Harrison wants to own me."

Moments later, Harrison James swept Jeanie into his arms. Quentin's insides twisted at how easy they had it. Jeanie had loved Harrison for years. What was it like to have such unswerving female devotion?

"Good thing I didn't cancel the wedding," his stepmother observed wryly.

He envied Harrison's confidence in his masculinity.

The man had no qualms about going down on his knees. He proposed to Jeanie again in front of the entire family. Harrison didn't have to live up to the heroic, larger-than-life image of Quentin Senior. Quentin worried about that every day.

As Jeanie's future once more resolved itself, his sister Lucy ventured, "Quentin, I've got the perfect woman for you."

He rolled his eyes. "Sorry, Luce. I'm out of the blind-date market."

"You'd be perfect together," Lucy insisted. "I know it."

Across the table, Alf and John howled with laughter. He scowled at them. Happily-ever-after was a myth perpetrated by fairy tales, florists, and greeting card companies. And jewelers. He couldn't forget them. "No. Four engagements are enough."

"There's someone out there for you, Quent." Her voice softened. "We'll find her."

"That's exactly what I'm afraid of." He carried an armload of dessert dishes to the kitchen. Stacking the dishes in the dishwasher calmed his thoughts.

After fiancée number four, Amy, dumped him, he'd decided that engagements gave women strange ideas. Ex number three, Janice Green, kept turning up at the oddest places. Apparently, she wanted him back. The feeling wasn't mutual.

He had no plans to date anyone, much less suffer through another catastrophic engagement. He'd suffered enough.

Then again, he wasn't sure he believed his own hype. Not with a certain sexy redhead haunting his thoughts.

CHAPTER THREE

"Nice of you to join us, Ms. Heartly."

Emma reminded herself that she needed this job. Responding to Joel's sarcasm in like form would be a mistake. "Sorry I'm late. Car trouble."

She forged stoically past her co-workers. The only vacant seat was beside her despicable boss at the head of the conference table. Glancing across the room, she made eye contact with her best friend, Dr. Lucy Sterling. Lucy also had a front-row seat.

Joel Frazier, CEO of Orbital Scientific, frowned his disapproval. "I'll see you in my office after the staff meeting, Ms. Heartly."

Emma's fake smile did not dim. She'd work around the clock on her bed and breakfast to get out from under this man's heavy thumb. "Yes, sir."

As her colleagues gave their weekly status reports, she listened with half an ear. The suck-ups elaborated; the cautious minced words.

She understood their caution. Joel Frazier lived for

information. The more he squeezed out of a person, the more he used it against them.

When Joel's aunt had offered her a job, Emma had been very grateful for the opportunity. She'd worked hard to keep her position. She still worked hard, but she found it difficult to be grateful after Joel had taken over the company from his aunt last year. Emma assumed nothing would change at Orbital. She should have known better.

Joel had used her ideas and enthusiasm to build his investment base. Although their professional relationship became personal, Emma believed she'd been promoted on the basis of merit, not because the boss had designs on her body.

She'd been so naive.

Joel called her his sounding board. He claimed it was natural for their professional relationship to turn intimate. Though he showered her with attention, she never quite bought into his worldview.

For one thing, he never shut up. For another, he always had to be right. Annoying faults, but still not enough to reveal the real Joel.

The way he vented his temper on his staff during his weekly staff meetings gave her a much truer perspective of his measure. Thank God, or right now she'd be in a worse mess. Joel had been wearing down her guard, slowly. She'd almost talked herself into believing the people he chewed out deserved it.

To think she'd almost been desperate enough to sleep with Joel.

Almost, but not quite.

Luckily she'd kept her eyes open—wide open.

She'd breezed into Joel's office one afternoon and found him occupied with his receptionist. Barb's state of undress spoke volumes about Joel's dedication to Emma.

That had been the end of Joel and Emma.

Since then, her worth within the company had plummeted. The ladder to corporate success had been yanked from her grasp.

"Emma?" Joel's voice cut into her daydreams.

She blinked her attention back to the conference room. Twelve pairs of eyes stared intently at her. It must be her turn to speak. She recited her progress report. "Sampling is on schedule. We currently have no backlog."

"Amazing. You have a talent for mundane work, Ms. Heartly." Joel's florid complexion matched his sarcastic tone.

A series of relieved chuckles swept through the room. Each week, Joel Frazier selected one of his employees to humiliate.

It must be her week. As it had been last week and the week before.

She managed a cool smile. "We all have our little talents, don't we, Mr. Frazier?"

The very earnest Herbert Goodlow cracked his pencil in half. "Excuse me," he mumbled, white-faced.

Emma hadn't paid attention to the man who had taken her old job of manager of Research and Development. Joel's late night, champagne-filled planning sessions, a requirement for the R&D manager, took on a whole new meaning. Glancing over at her colleague, she inwardly cringed at the fierce glare he shot at her.

"No problem, Herb. I can afford to keep you in pencils." Joel turned back to Emma. "Share with us, Ms. Heartly, how you accomplished this miraculous feat?"

She translated his request to mean he planned on her failure. Everyone knew that sample volume increased during the summer months. Problems arose every year because staff members took vacations during that time. But she'd found a way to make it work. She wouldn't give the man the satisfaction of sloppy work to degrade her with.

She was tired of pretending she cared about her train wreck of a job. Even more tired of pretending she didn't care about Joel using her for target practice, Emma leveled her gaze at her boss. "The credit goes to you, Mr. Frazier. You selected the right woman for the job."

For a moment, Emma thought she'd gone deaf. Nobody breathed. Nobody moved.

Joel snapped his appointment book shut. "Well then, that's all for today."

Emma rose with everyone else, intending to drop off her purse in the lab before meeting with Joel. She'd lost her office with her demotion. Now her personal space consisted of a small area of counter she'd hacked out for herself in the corner of the sampling lab.

Lucy Sterling caught up with her in the corridor. "You're breathing fire this morning. Get up on the wrong side of someone's bed?"

Emma arched an eyebrow. Lucy believed love made the world go around. She kept badgering Emma to walk on the wild side. "You know the status of my love life. My bed is the only one I'm sleeping in."

Lucy's cheek twitched. "It must have killed Joel when you wouldn't sleep with him."

Her reckless mood flared again. "The man doesn't need a girlfriend. His universe consists of him, his desires, and his needs. Don't get me started on Joel."

Lucy laughed. "But it's so fun to get you wound up."

"We need to work on your definition of fun." Emma entered the Sampling Lab.

Lucy cocked her head in interest. "Have something in mind?"

"How about a weekend in the country?" Emma stuffed her purse in a laboratory drawer. "I can guarantee you will be thoroughly exhausted on Monday morning."

"Sounds great. I assume you mean this weekend?"

Emma nodded. "Are you available?"

"Sure, I'd love to get out of town. But only if you agree to hear me out about my brother."

She recognized the determined glint in her friend's eyes. For weeks, Lucy had been trying to interest Emma in her brother. The last thing Emma needed right now was a blind date. But if Lucy helped her with the renovation, she would owe Lucy. She always paid her debts. "Deal."

She'd worry about Lucy's brother later. Right now she had a much more immediate problem down the hall. No telling what Joel wanted. "If you'll excuse me, I'll continue to indulge in my professional suicide."

Lucy snorted. "You're a moneymaker. *He* would be committing professional suicide if he fired you. Sampling was a disaster before you took over. Everything you touch turns to gold."

Emma shot her friend a telling glance. "Knowing is one thing, understanding is another. The man believes we're all disposable."

"Why do you think I'm such a big suck-up?" Lucy batted her long eyelashes.

"Lucy, you could charm the skin off a snake. Joel knows he can't manipulate you. Speaking of our boss,

I've gotta run."

With haste, Emma traversed the hall. She wished she had Lucy's fortitude. She had a sinking feeling that she'd give in to Joel's bullying rather than be fired.

She didn't deserve his foul mood. She'd done nothing wrong, but Joel saw it differently. In his eyes, she was guilty for not overlooking his infidelity. Her defiance cost her a pay grade. He'd further punished her by demoting her to Sample Processing.

Why should she continue to accept the crap he dumped on her? He'd cheated on her, not the other way around. If only he wasn't her boss.

She knocked on Joel's office door.

"Enter."

With her heart in her throat, Emma stepped inside. Joel's oversized ebony desk dominated the room. Its sleek modern lines contrasted with the antiques lining the ivory-colored walls.

She stood behind his guest chairs. She wouldn't dream of sitting without his permission.

Why had she ever dated this control freak? She didn't care for his artificial tan or bleached blond hair. He was fake inside and out.

A shell of a man really.

No, that wasn't right. A shell implied that something had once been inside his thick hide.

He was a parody of a man. She recently had firsthand experience of what a real man acted like. Joel Frazier did not begin to measure up to Quentin Stone. Joel was not a solid man of action. Joel would never put her safety before his.

What did he want? Private humiliation wasn't his style. Was there something more devious, more sinister up his sleeve? She fortified her nerves with gulps of scared rabbit courage.

"Ms. Heartly, I'm sure you know why I called you in here," he began after considerable time had passed.

"Actually, I don't." Emma pretended her job wasn't on the line.

"I expect my department heads to be role models. It's a poor reflection on the company when a department head is tardy."

He'd summoned her for this? She swallowed a bark of laughter. "I'm sorry, sir. It won't happen again."

He smiled at her in a patronizing manner. "Please have a seat."

She perched on the edge of a chair.

"I can't be lenient with you, Emma. People would think our personal relationship gave you special privileges."

Her heart missed a beat. They didn't have a personal relationship. "Mr. Frazier. I apologized for coming in late. A dead battery is not a routine occurrence, it rarely happens." A cold chill seeped into her bones. "And, for the record, we don't have a personal relationship."

He walked around his desk emoting concern. "You've had time to get over your upset. Men have needs that must be met. Barb meant nothing to me. Stop this foolishness. Come to dinner with me tomorrow night."

"I'm not going out with you. How much clearer can I be?"

He sighed sadly. "I need you. I'm entertaining potential investors. I want you at my side."

Her mouth tightened. How dare he think he could command her to go out with him? She wasn't a robot. He'd trampled all over her feelings. "Isn't that what the head of R&D is supposed to do? Schmooze the clients with you? It must have slipped your mind that I'm no longer in R&D. I'm in Sample Processing. Your R&D chief should attend the dinner meeting."

His gaze narrowed. "It isn't the same. I need *you*. No one can talk shop to these people like you can. They want to hear your excitement."

She didn't believe him. "There are ten other highly qualified individuals in this company capable of attending a business dinner with you. People with PhDs."

"I don't want any of the others." His voice dropped to a lower register, one that used to give her chills. "I want you. We look good together. The clients go for that united front kind of thing."

He wasn't listening to her. Maybe he would get it if she tried some of his logic on him. "If I went out with you, people would assume I slept my way back into your good graces. Your R&D chief would feel threatened. Definitely bad for corporate morale."

"You're not changing my mind." Joel leveled his index finger at her. "I'll spell it out in plain English. Your job depends on your attendance. I'm ordering you to appear."

Emma swallowed thickly. So much for being a free-spirited child of the universe. She couldn't afford her rehab if she lost this job. Her only option was to cave. "Yes, sir."

Great. She didn't need this. She could have gone the rest of her life without spending another moment with Joel. "Where do I meet you?"

"I'll pick you up at seven."

Alarm flashed through her body. "I'm not your date. I'll provide my own transportation. Where are we meeting your clients for dinner?"

His hand flew up to ward off her flurry of words. "All right. I concede. Meet me at my country club at seven fifteen."

She'd given him what she wanted. Now she needed to set the ground rules. "Let's make sure there are no misunderstandings here. I'm doing this because my job is on the line. I'm not your girlfriend. If you lay a finger on me, I'm walking out."

"That wasn't so hard, was it?" Joel's icy smile turned her stomach. "You did the right thing. We're a team. You're dismissed."

On the way to the sampling lab, Emma reviewed the conversation. Joel needed her? Impossible. Even more impossible was his insistence they were a team.

She'd never trust him again.

* * *

Quentin didn't look at the phone on his desk. He shuffled through the pile of invoices again. Everything tallied. He could take a break now. Even though he couldn't see the phone, Emma's phone number whispered in his ear.

With gunslinger quickness, he palmed the receiver and punched up the number from memory.

What was he doing?

He hung up.

He leaned back in his office chair in disgust. Without a reason to call, he'd sound like a star-struck teen. Something flittered at the edge of his thoughts. If he could come up with a legitimate reason, he'd call her.

"What's her name?" John asked.

Quentin lifted his gaze to the doorway where his brother leered at him.

"Who is she?" his brother persisted.

He rose to his feet and shoved his hands in his pockets. "What makes you think this is about a woman?"

"You can't fool me, big brother. I know you too well." John grinned. "A woman has captured your attention. Have you set a wedding date?"

Quentin stumbled over the word date. They hadn't even been on a date. He'd very much like to hold Emma's hand, to see her lips part with a smile for him. "No."

John leaned against the doorframe. Quentin wasn't fooled by his brother's casual stance. "Are you bringing her to Sunday dinner this week?" John asked.

"No." Quentin recoiled at the thought of exposing his reluctant fascination with Emma to his entire family.

"Interesting." John absently scratched his chin. "You aren't normally indecisive about women. You see one you want. You go after her. None of this dithering around."

He couldn't deny the truth. In the past, he'd pushed women hard to commit to him early in a relationship, but he knew firsthand how nonbinding engagements were. He wouldn't repeat that mistake again.

"Is it Lucy's scientist friend?" John asked.

Quentin paced his office. "You don't know her. I'm changing my strategy with this woman. My track record with dating isn't the best, you know."

"Maybe I can help," his brother offered. "What sort of strategy are we talking about?"

"Mostly I'm doing the opposite of everything I've done in the past."

"From the pained expression on your face, I'd say it isn't working." John laughed. "Are you sure roses and candlelit dinners wouldn't help?"

"I'm not sure about anything." He stopped pacing to stare at the first stars of the evening. "All I know is that I can't stop thinking about her."

"So? What's the problem?"

He exhaled deeply. "She thinks I'm bossy."

His brother's laughter echoed down the hall.

* * *

The next evening, Joel walked Emma to her car after the business dinner. "That went well," Joel said. "You had Robert Galway eating out of the palm of your hand."

Emma's hospitable facade faded. Dinner lasted two lifetimes. Now she wanted to go home. "The evening is over. I have a long drive ahead of me."

"And why is that?" He matched her step for step.

"I moved." She fumbled in her purse for her keys.

"Oh? Be sure to update your personnel records at Orbital."

"I'll do that." Emma sat in her Volvo. "Good night."

He scanned the contents of her car. She cursed her bad fortune for parking under a streetlight. His X-ray vision inspected every gum wrapper on her floor mats. He caught the door, keeping her from closing it.

His sickly sweet cologne penetrated her car, fouling the air. "Won't you give us another chance? Don't you remember how good we were together?"

Rancor sharpened her voice. "A certain indiscretion in your office comes to mind when I think of our time together."

"You can't hold that against me forever."

"Wanna bet?"

"You don't fool me. You're playing hard to get."

"Grow up, Joel. We're through." As long as he thought she was available, he would nag her to go out with him again. Time to stretch the truth a bit. "I'm interested in someone else now."

She held her breath while Joel absorbed her message. His eyes narrowed. He stepped back from the car. Relief coursed through her as she drove home. She'd survived. Even better, she'd rebuffed his attention without losing her job.

She sagged into her seat, mentally weary and physically drained. Tonight could have been spent working on the farmhouse. Instead, she'd spent her free time with her boss, a man she despised.

Too bad she wouldn't see Quentin Stone ever again. In the ten minutes of her acquaintance with him, he'd shown more gentlemanly qualities than Joel had in a year. Joel was all about Joel, he'd never been devoted to her.

Grandma had been right about men like Joel. A man you couldn't trust was worthless. The further she distanced herself from Joel, the better she felt.

At home, her step quickened at the blinking light on her answering machine. For a moment, she hoped Quentin had called. That he'd been so impressed by her beauty and charm he couldn't stay away.

Fat chance. Quentin wouldn't have any trouble getting a date, anytime, anywhere. He probably had a black book full of phone numbers of suitable women.

She listened to her message. "Emma? It's Beverly. Nothing urgent, but I'd like to talk to you about the house. Give me a call or come by when you're free."

Was Beverly coming around to her way of thinking? If she had Beverly, she was halfway to her goal. Only this was an all or nothing proposition. She needed both of her sisters' signatures on that Quit Claim Deed or she wouldn't have a clear title.

How on earth would she change Maddy's mind?

CHAPTER FOUR

On Saturday morning, Quentin slowed for the turn into Emma's lane. He'd awakened with an overwhelming urgency to see her. The need had grown with every passing second, propelling him to take action.

He had to see her.

What if she'd been baking again? Averting her kitchen fire last week had left an indelible impression on him. Now he yearned to see her.

Was she as vivid, engaging and headstrong as he remembered? Was that jolt of current he'd felt when they touched a product of his imagination?

He had to know.

Gravel crunched under his tires. He probably should have called first. But he'd come unannounced. Her zippy little compact and a battered Volvo were parked in the yard. The Maryland tag on the Volvo read LUCY1.

His sister's car.

What was Lucy doing here?

How did she know Emma Heartly?

If Lucy breathed a word about this visit to the family, he would find himself engaged in a heartbeat. He would be very careful how he acted around his matchmaking sister. There would be no need for Lucy to report him to the engagement police.

Besides, he finally remembered an excuse for being here. He'd inadvertently left his clipboard behind. As head of Stone Construction, he had a responsibility to recover company property. If Lucy questioned his visit, he'd trot out that story for her.

The early morning sun lightened the weathered gray of the Victorian farmhouse. Though the place needed lots of work, he loved the old-fashioned elegance of the dwelling. It would be a thrill to restore this place.

As he mounted the creaking stairs, he noticed Emma's pets peering in the screen door. They turned at his approach, the cat walking over to bump against his leg. He patted the dog on the head and glanced through the screen to the eerily silent house.

The sense of wrongness intensified the urgency circling his veins. There was no sign of movement, no hint of habitation. "Emma? Lucy?"

No answer.

He battled the rising tide of concern to think this through. They could be in the back yard. He should circle the house before he leapt to any conclusions. His gut didn't agree with his head.

He sniffed the air for smoke, but the air smelled country fresh. His pulse quickened. A reckless, headstrong woman like Emma probably needed a keeper. He wanted to apply for the position. But he had to find her first.

He called out again, louder, "Emma? Lucy?"

He tried the door.

Locked.

Why didn't they answer? The sense of wrongness overwhelmed his innate caution.

Without further thought, he punched through the screen door to gain entrance into the house. "Emma? Lucy?" He immediately noticed the yawning hole in the living room floor by the window. That was not completely unexpected given the dry rot he had noted in the floorboards.

A chill shivered down his spine.

He edged closer to the jagged opening. Two crumpled figures lay amid the rubble in the basement. "Oh, my God. Emma? Lucy?"

No response. The shortest way to them was straight down. He needed a rope and a flashlight. Both were in his Jeep.

Moments later, he stood in the basement rubble. Sawdust clogged his nostrils. Rotted wood littered the floor. He feared the worst and hoped for the best as he aimed the beam of light on his stepsister.

No blood.

That was good.

Her upper body appeared trauma-free, but her swollen ankle indicated trouble. "Luce? Answer me. You all right?" He stroked her face gently to revive her.

Her eyes opened slowly. "Quentin."

"What happened?"

She tried to sit up but cried out in pain. She slumped back to the floor. "The floor collapsed. We were prying out the bad boards when the whole darn floor collapsed. Where's Emma?"

He gave her hand a reassuring squeeze. "Don't

move. I'll check on her."

He climbed over a plaid sofa littered with hunks of flooring to reach Emma. His mouth turned dry at the six-by-six floor joist inches from her head. Chips of wood dotted her body.

The air stilled in his lungs at her lifeless form.

She couldn't be dead. He would not accept that outcome. He scanned her length. Her chest rose and fell in small increments, easing the tightness in his ribs.

She was alive.

He smoothed the silky hair back from her pale face. "Emma? Wake up."

Her eyelashes fluttered, setting off butterflies in his stomach. She blinked her eyes open. At the bright light, her eyelids closed. His heart sunk at the sight of her large pupils. Concussion most likely.

He diverted the flashlight beam away from her pale face. Where before her expression had been so animated, now it appeared devoid of expression, inciting his worry.

His fingers trailed down the side of her face. He leaned in close. The delightful aroma of wildflowers assailed him, blinding him to everything but the universe of Emma. She had to be all right. He willed her eyes to open again.

She blinked, and relief swept through him, overwhelming his inhibitions. He touched his lips to hers. "Emma? Do you know who I am?"

She nodded, wincing at the slight motion.

Her response staunched the worst of his concerns, but he wouldn't feel better until both women received medical attention. "Be still. I'm calling for help." He unclipped his mobile phone from his belt and made the call.

No signal.

"Stay put. I'll be right back." From the porch, he contacted emergency services.

What else could he do to help?

He knew not to move them, although it couldn't be comfortable on that concrete floor. Warmth. That's what they needed. He could wrap them in blankets. He grabbed blankets from the upstairs beds, tossing them down into the hole before he climbed down the rope.

He covered Lucy first. "Help is on its way, Luce."

"Th-thanks," she managed through chattering teeth.

"What are you doing here?" he asked. An answer popped into his head. "Let me guess. Emma is your scientist friend?"

"Yes," Lucy answered softly.

"Hang in there. I'm going to cover Emma."

He scaled the sofa with the other blanket draped over his shoulder. To his dismay, Emma was standing. "Wait a minute. A doctor needs to examine you." She swayed. He steadied her shoulders, his pulse racing at her nearness.

She swatted at his hands. "I'm all right except for a headache. How's Lucy?"

"Her ankle is swollen. What happened?"

"We were prying out the bad floorboards. I heard wood splintering." She clutched her arms to her chest. "One minute we were in the living room, the next we were falling."

While holding her, he gazed at the gaping hole overhead. "This is what happens when amateurs do rehabs. You two could have broken your necks."

She clutched her head. "Don't yell at me. I'm injured."

He had no right to yell, no right to care. But that

hadn't stopped him from doing either one. "Sorry. I brought you a blanket." He draped it around her shoulders.

Her shivering didn't abate, so he gently enfolded her into his arms. To his delight, she nestled against him, her curves fitting into his hollows. "Help will be here soon."

He let out a shaky breath. If he hadn't acted on impulse this morning, no telling how long it would have taken for someone to find them. But he had come. And help was on the way.

The dog howled in concert with the approaching sirens. Emma struggled to stand independently. "Don't even think about it, Red." His arms tightened protectively around her. "You're staying put until the paramedics check you." He guided them over to the sofa and drew her into his lap.

The cloud of her curly hair tickled his nose as she rested her head on his shoulder. Though he didn't have the right, he wanted to kiss her again. A real kiss this time.

She huffed out a breath of air. "Sheesh. You don't handle stress well. Have you ever tried meditation?"

He glared at her. Didn't she realize her disregard for her safety had triggered his distress?

She lifted her head and met his steely gaze with feminine challenge. "I guess that means no. You should take a class in it. Or yoga. Or massage therapy."

Quentin snorted. The woman was definitely off her rocker. The day he set foot in a yoga class would be the end of his authority over his construction crews. "Real men don't need stress reduction."

Emma laughed and then grabbed her head. "Ow. Don't make me laugh."

His clasped arms encircled her waist. He liked being close to her. The color was back in her cheeks, but she wasn't one hundred percent by any means.

"I'm guessing from the conversation that you've already met my brother," Lucy said.

"Your brother?" Emma studied his face. "You don't look anything alike. And you have different last names."

His frustration mounted with each passing second. Neither woman comprehended the gravity of the situation. No one would have checked on them until Monday when they didn't show up for work.

"Blended family," Lucy said. "My Mom married his Dad. Quentin and I are from their respective first marriages."

"I had no idea." Emma shook her head. "You're so nice, Lucy. How come he's so bossy?"

"Quentin is not quite himself. I've never seen him this way before."

"Hey, I'm in the room," he said. "Don't talk about me like I'm not here."

Emma's gaze traveled from sister to brother. "You mean he never loses his temper?"

"Never." His sister's voice rang with certainty.

"He never yells at anyone else?"

"Only at family. He always treats his women like crystal."

Emma punched him playfully in the stomach. "Who are you? What have you done with Lucy's brother?"

"Easy, Red," he murmured in her curly hair.

"How long have you two been dating?" Lucy asked.

"We aren't dating," Quentin interjected before his sister brought up his women again. He didn't want her to know he'd struck out four times. "I met her last week when I came out to give an estimate. Things got a little confused, and I left my clipboard here."

"Confused? How?" Lucy asked.

His sister would hound him until she had the details. Better to deflect her with a bit more of the truth. "Emma set her oven on fire. She ran into a smoke-filled kitchen to fight the fire. Satisfied?"

Lucy inhaled sharply. "Fire? No wonder things got confused. Wait until I tell the others."

He shot Lucy a quelling glance. "There's nothing to tell."

"Hello. Anybody in here?" a male voice called from above.

A wave of relief washed through Quentin. "Down here. Careful of the floor. When it gave way, the women fell through. One has a busted ankle. The other may have a concussion."

Once the paramedics gained the basement, Quentin reluctantly let Emma go. He shoved his hands in his pockets to keep from reaching for her again. The honeysuckle aroma of her hair lingered in his head. She smiled at the paramedic, and jealousy bit him hard. He wanted all of her smiles, too.

He groaned at the realization.

So much for taking it slow with this woman.

* * *

At the hospital, his sister insisted on Quentin notifying their entire family, which he did. Conversely, Emma didn't want him to call anyone. Worry creased his brow. She didn't have to be alone over there.

He considered telling the head nurse that Emma was

his fiancée, but he didn't want his family getting any ideas when they arrived. He prowled his sister's cubicle.

Lucy caught his eye. "Emma's different, isn't she?"

"Different?" Loud footfalls sounded on the tile floor. He peeked out of the curtain in time to see men in white coats exit Emma's area. They walked right past him. He sighed and reluctantly focused on his sister's question. "She's headstrong, reckless, and bossy. She has no regard for her personal safety."

"Woo-hoo," Lucy crowed. "I knew you two would be perfect together. She's what you need. No more plastic women."

"I'd appreciate it if the entire family would get off my back about the whole dating thing. I barely know Emma. We aren't dating."

"Right. I saw how you looked at her."

"What did you see?"

Her gaze softened. "I saw a man holding a woman as if she were the rarest treasure on the earth."

"Time to get your contact lens prescription changed," he scoffed. "I helped my sister and her friend."

"Oh, Quentin, it was more than that."

Her wistful voice pierced his heart. He was a sap but that was his secret. "Women view the world through rosy glasses. Men don't see things that way. We see facts. Here's the relevant fact in this case, Emma is a beautiful woman. Does that satisfy you?"

Lucy smiled smugly. "I wasn't sure you noticed, what with all the confusion."

"I noticed all right." He paced the small cubicle.

What was taking so long with Emma?

CHAPTER FIVE

"There's a hunk across the corridor who keeps looking over here," the nurse said. She checked Emma's blood pressure again. "Is he your boyfriend?"

Quentin's hands had been on her back, waist, and head. His lips had touched hers, causing her heart to beat double time even now. Racing hearts were undesirable in the Emergency Room.

If her blood pressure spiked, they'd keep her longer. "He's a friend."

"Shall I invite him over?"

From her suggestive tone, it seemed the nurse wanted to invite Quentin to dinner. Emma had the distinct impression he wanted more than dinner from her. The way his arms had snugged her up to his muscular torso had been wonderful.

Maybe too wonderful.

But she needed help getting out of here. "Sure."

With a coy smile on her face, the nurse escorted Quentin into the small cubicle. The sight of him cheered

Emma more than she wanted to admit.

Worry lines bracketed his mouth. He touched her arm. Warmth and compassion radiated up her limb. "You okay?"

The huskiness in his voice warmed the arctic chill from her veins. His pleasant outdoor scent, a mixture of Quentin and sunshine and a spring breeze, filled her lungs. She took another deep breath. Why had he kissed her?

She shrugged off the distracting thoughts. "I'm fine." A crowd of people started talking all at once in the hallway. The noise aggravated her headache, made her stomach roil. She frowned at the unpleasant sensations.

"What did the doctors say?" he asked.

"Same thing you said. Concussion." She sat up on the gurney. A wave of dizziness swamped her. "I'm going home now. Would you call me a cab?"

"I'll drive you. What about paperwork?"

The noise outside intensified. Her head throbbed. The curtained walls seemed to close in on her, choking the air from her lungs. She had to get out of here. "They've already had me sign my life away."

"Home it is." Quentin pulled back the curtain. A wall of people engulfed them.

Emma heard the petite blonde ask Lucy, "Is this your friend from work?"

The strangers milled around Lucy's wheelchair. Emma's heart panged at the thick bandage on Lucy's ankle. She threaded her way to her friend's side. "I'm so sorry."

"Everyone, this is my friend Emma," Lucy said.

"Hi, Emma," came the group reply.

Her head pounded at the volume. She shrunk back

away from the crowd, right into Quentin. At the full-body contact she startled. He steadied her, bringing a stream of heat up her neck to her face. "Hi."

Lucy made introductions. The names swirled like a kaleidoscope. Tabby. Alf. Jeanie. John. Dottie. Emma tried to remember the names but there were too many of them.

The white-haired woman with the red scarf engulfed Emma in a hug. "You poor thing. Lucy told me all about the accident."

Emma thought that was Dottie, but she wasn't sure. She retreated into Quentin. Her fingers sought his. Relief flared through her at his comforting touch.

"I'm so sorry," she repeated. "I need to go home."

The beefy guy stepped forward. "I'll take you home."

The younger man dressed in black stepped forward, too. "Let me. I'd love to take you home."

She reeled from the conversational volleyball. There were so many of them, so many loud voices, so many bright colors. She shielded her eyes with her hand.

"You guys are scaring her," the brunette cautioned with a wave of her hand. The diamond on her ring flashed at the rapid movement. "Can't you see that this situation calls for a woman's sensitivity? I'll drive her home."

"I'm taking Emma home," Quentin announced in a no-nonsense tone. "John, you and Alf make sure Lucy has what she needs at her place."

Amid a chorus of goodbyes, he navigated her into his Jeep. As the chaos abated, the pounding in her head lessened. "Thanks," she said, snapping her seat belt in place.

"My family can be overwhelming."

"Mmm." The motion of the vehicle disoriented her. Nausea hit her hard. She closed her eyes to get her bearings.

"I'll call your family when we get you home," Quentin offered. "You need someone to stay with you today."

"I can manage." Her sisters would use the accident against her. They would lobby hard for her to return to the city. She couldn't take that chance.

"You shouldn't be alone. Concussions are serious."

So were sisters.

Her temper flared. "I've got a gaping hole in my floor, an expensive hospital bill, and an injured best friend. What makes you think I need company?"

"You have medical insurance. Quit complaining."

She snorted. "Orbital's health insurance carries a five-thousand-dollar deductible. I shouldn't have gone to the hospital. I'm out the entire cost of the visit."

He held her gaze a moment longer than necessary. "You're not going to make me feel guilty for insisting you be checked out after that fall. I grew up in a house full of females. I know all about guilt."

She scowled at him. "What about your Dad? Didn't he put a stop to that?"

"Dad died in a fire."

The steel in his voice lanced through her, riddling her with guilt. "I'm sorry." Why did she push for answers? Why couldn't she accept what people said on face value?

"And your family?" he asked.

Uncomfortable with his line of inquiry, she chewed her lip. "My family is smaller than yours."

"Tell me about them."

"My sisters, Maddy and Beverly, are all the family I have. Every one else is dead. Dead, dead, dead." She held her throbbing head in her hands. Family matters stressed her in the best of times. They were a real killer with a mild concussion. "I don't want to talk about my family."

"Okay."

Her head pounded. Her stomach ached. Heat and chills flashed through her, leaving behind clammy skin. Her abdomen clenched. "Stop the car," she whispered.

Quentin slowed. Her body temperature soared. Sweat rolled down the center of her back. She gripped the door handle. The world tilted on its axis.

Her stomach heaved. She lunged from the Jeep, walked two paces, and threw up on her shoes. Strong hands supported her shoulders until the nausea subsided.

She swallowed hard. Death would be easier to face than this queasy humiliation. She stared at her shoes. How could she get back in his Jeep smelling like vomit?

Why didn't she carry breath mints? "I'm sorry."

"It's all right. You've had a rough day."

She hugged herself, shivering at the undeserved kindness in his voice. "I'm such a mess. I can't get back in your vehicle. I'll walk the rest of the way home."

"Don't be ridiculous." He steered her into his Jeep. "It's easily fifteen miles to your house."

His continued kindness set her off. "I don't deserve your help. I'm the reason your sister got hurt, for goodness sake. Don't you blame me?"

He drove with the windows rolled down. "Lucy is a big girl. I doubt I could have kept her away if she decided to stay with you this weekend. I don't blame you for her injury, but I hold you responsible for injuring yourself."

She shrugged. "Stuff happens."

"*Stuff* seems to follow you around."

She didn't like his tone of voice. Her chin shot up. "Everyone has accidents."

"You knew that floor was bad. That demolition needed to be handled by a professional."

Tears welled in her eyes. Her head thundered. "I didn't know it was that bad. I feel awful about the accident."

He exhaled slowly. "I'm sorry. I didn't mean to raise my voice."

Right.

Emma wished she could start this day over. She hadn't wanted to be glad to see Quentin again. She hadn't wanted him to hold her like he cared for her.

But his arms had felt strong. Protective.

He'd expressed concern over her well-being. That meant something. People that didn't care wouldn't do that. Which left the alternative. He cared for her. That knowledge ignited a tiny spark of hope inside, making her feel cherished.

He was the sexiest man she'd ever met. His heroic actions loomed larger than life. Twice now he'd rescued her from dangerous situations. That would be enough to turn any woman's head. That and his kiss. She'd have given a week's vacation to know why he kissed her.

She blamed her vulnerability on the unusual circumstances. She was self-sufficient. She had looked after her family for years. She was darn near invincible.

That claim made her snort with laughter.

"Excuse me?"

She clamped a hand over her mouth. "Sorry. I had a silly thought."

"And?"

And she planned on keeping it to herself. Noting that his car had stopped in her driveway, Emma cleared her throat. "Thanks for all you've done. I can take it from here."

He intercepted her before she closed the car door. "I'm not leaving until your sisters arrive."

"I don't want them here. I don't need anyone bossing me around."

She kicked off her smelly shoes in the yard, stepped over the dog, and ascended the porch steps. "I have a headache and I don't feel like being nice. Go home."

"You won't even know I'm here."

She barely managed to curtail her snort of disbelief. His every exhalation caught her notice. "I appreciate everything you've done for me, but I'm not up for company."

"I'm staying. You shouldn't be alone."

She ignored him. That worked until he reached around her to open the screen door, a sheepish grin on his face. "Sorry about the hole in your screen. I got excited when you didn't answer my knock. I'll replace the screen."

"Yes, you will. The plan is to fix this place up, not hasten its demise." The thought of Quentin returning to fix her door cheered her considerably. The pounding in her head subsided.

He steered her toward the stairs. "Your bedroom is on the second floor, right?"

"That's right." Her thoughts weren't about resting. They centered on the virile man at her heels. The man intent on visiting her bedroom.

The heat radiating from his palm centered on the small of her back warmed her like a Bunsen burner. She needed a refuge to cool off.

"Excuse me." She ducked into the upstairs bathroom and closed the door.

Emma splashed her face with cold water. She brushed her teeth. Much better. She felt like herself for the first time in hours. So much better that she didn't want to spend the day in bed, thinking about kissing her rescuer.

Weekends were precious chunks of time. If she lounged around, this place would never be a bed and breakfast.

She opened the door, brushed past Quentin, and hustled downstairs.

"Where do you think you're going?"

"I got the medical check-up you wanted." She tossed her words over her shoulder. "Now I'm doing what I want. I've got too much work to do to sit around."

He trailed after her. "You're supposed to take it easy today."

"I appreciate your concern, but I'm fine."

She glanced around the dark house trying to figure out what to do. With her headache, demolition wasn't a good choice. She had bought more barn paint. That sounded safe enough. She headed out the back door.

He matched her quickened stride. "You just checked out of the hospital. If you hit your head again, you might cause permanent injury."

"Then I won't hit my head." She stooped to pick up the paint can, and another twinge of nausea assailed her. With determination, she gritted through the disorientation.

"You shouldn't be up doing things."

Her patience wore thin. "I know you mean well, but

I've been looking after myself for years. If you're determined to stay, please respect my decision. Or help me paint. I could always use an extra pair of hands."

In silence, he grabbed a brush and painted a perfect square of paint on the boards. His precision annoyed her. She slapped a brush full of red paint on the side of the barn. "Do you have to do it that way?"

His brows knit together. "Is something wrong?"

Everything was wrong.

The crappy day.

The pounding head.

The bossy man.

No wonder she was grumpy. "It's going to take all day that way."

"We've got all day. Unless you have another harebrained demolition scheme in mind."

He didn't sound calm. In fact, he sounded downright agitated. Curious, she turned to him. "What are you doing here?"

He continued to paint precise squares on her barn. "I'm keeping an eye on you. Doctor's orders."

His answer didn't ring true. "Not that. I meant, why did you come here today?"

"I left my clipboard here the other day." He hesitated. "Today was the first chance I had to retrieve it."

Her hopes deflated. "Oh."

"Don't you know why I came?" His husky voice curled her toes. "I wanted to see you again."

Her lips parted.

Her headache receded.

Would he kiss her again?

What was she doing? Heartlys didn't get happily-ever-after endings.

She busied herself dipping her brush in the paint. Under cover of her eyelashes, she observed Quentin's stillness. If she said anything, he'd think she was a nut.

Who wouldn't? He made her happy and miserable, hopeful and desolate.

"Don't leave me hanging, Red. Say something."

Should she tell him her family history? Or about Joel? "I'm a chicken."

Oops.

Did she really say that out loud?

"Women who run into smoking kitchens aren't chickens. Tell me what you're thinking. Is there someone else?"

"No one. I mean I'm not seeing anyone." Emma averted her eyes from his penetrating stare. She hadn't had a sexual relationship since college. She'd been too busy to fit a man into her schedule. "I had a relationship that ended badly. I'm done with being chopped liver."

He leaned toward her. "Chopped liver? What's this guy's name? I'll be glad to adjust his attitude for you."

She met his intent gaze and laughed aloud. "Like beat him up or something?"

"Or something." His eyes sparkled with danger.

"Don't tempt me. Joel might think I cared if I had him beat up."

"Joel, eh?"

She bit her bottom lip. "You caught that." Expectation rolled around her. "Joel Frazier is my boss. I still work for him, so don't beat him up."

"He sounds like a creep." Quentin scowled. "Why work for a man like that?"

Her spine stiffened. Why couldn't he accept what

she'd shared without being critical? "I don't need a solution. Joel is part of my past."

"I want to help."

"I don't need help, and I don't need another conscience."

He painted another perfect square. "I suggest we change the subject."

"What about books? Do you read?"

"I like action adventure stories," he answered. "What about you?"

"Romantic suspense. I like love stories with happy endings."

"Sounds a little hokey. Give me an international thriller any day."

"We don't agree on reading material either," she said.

He shrugged. "What's a little disagreement among friends?"

Emma connected her drips of paint. Quentin had been a good friend today. Too bad she wasn't in the market for a friend. Or in the market for a man whose deep, rumbling voice made her forget about financial independence.

CHAPTER SIX

Quentin ran the screen tool over the mesh fabric, locking the material solidly in the aluminum frame. Nice and tight, a perfect installation. "All done."

Emma bustled out of the house with a tray of sandwiches. She deposited the tray on the wooden bench. "So soon? That didn't take any time. How'd you do that?"

"Work goes fast with the right tools."

She flushed prettily. That splash of color encouraged him and added to the sense of well-being he felt around her.

"I have plenty of tools, but I couldn't have fixed that screen door in a month of Sundays. Too bad I can't afford to hire Stone Construction. With you around here, my rehab would get done just like that." She snapped her fingers.

Her remark gave him the opening he needed. He leaned up against the side of the house with studied casualness, his calm at odds with the blood swiftly pulsing through his eardrums. So much depended on his choosing the right words. "I've been thinking. I could give you a hand with your rehab but not on company time. It would have to be after hours."

She gulped air. "You'd help me? For nothing? Why would you do such a thing?"

"I love old houses. This one has great bones. I'd love to work on it. I'd also like to make sure you don't have any more trips to the Emergency Room." Because I want to spend time with you should have topped his explanations, but he didn't want to scare her off with that much honesty.

No point in mentioning he wanted to sleep with her either.

"Hey, the Emergency Room was your idea."

He held up his hand in protest. "We've had this discussion before. Your safety is important, and I want to help with the rehab."

A painful silence followed. He hung by a slim thread over a sheer drop. Everything inside of him stilled while he waited for her answer. He entertained thoughts of begging.

"Okay."

He exhaled slowly. "No arguments?"

"Hey, it's win-win for both of us. You want to work on old houses. I need this house renovated." She gestured toward the stack of sandwiches. "Dinner is served."

He returned his tools to his toolbox. "Thanks. I'd like to wash up first, if I may?"

"Sure." She gestured towards the house. "The first floor bathroom is down the hall on the left."

Quentin sauntered through the house. Emma had agreed to his offer of help, so he'd spend time with her.

Of course, she'd get her house redone in the meantime, but he didn't mind donating his skills. He liked this old house.

He liked her.

Definitely win-win for both of them.

He attended to business in the bathroom. Fast and furious had been his style with women. That practice had yielded four failed engagements. In the past, he'd gone after marriage the same way he approached a rehab. He'd marshaled his forces in an all-out barrage, wowing women into agreeing to marry him. But somewhere along the line, his engagements always derailed.

Clearly, he needed a new strategy.

Like the laid-back approach he was taking with Emma. Nothing fast or furious. Just a little construction here and there. Slow and deliberate, like refinishing an antique cabinet. If he concentrated on his love of old houses, then the romance wouldn't blindside him. This time he'd have both eyes open as he wooed her into his arms.

Returning to the spacious front porch, he joined Emma on the stairs. He eased down next to her and opened a can of iced tea. "What's for dinner?"

She shoved the tray at him. "I wasn't sure how hungry you would be. I made two peanut butter sandwiches for me and three for you. If you're still hungry afterward I can make more."

At least she wasn't cooking. He ate a bite of a peanut butter sandwich. "What would you like to work on first?"

She chuckled. "I know this place is in bad shape, but don't you think the hole in my floor is a top priority?"

He considered the problem as he chewed and swallowed. "I haven't forgotten your living room, but fixing that floor will require a substantial financial outlay for supplies." He paused to reach for a second sandwich, feeling his way through the treacherous maze of building a relationship. "I, uh, assumed your finances for this project are somewhat limited."

She flushed a deep red. "You assumed correctly."

"Even with my builder's discount, those supplies would be costly. I'm guessing there's some damage to the floor supports by the window. Those joists aren't cheap. Your great grandfather used six-by-six beams on twenty-four-inch centers. I could mend the supports by sistering a two-by-six to the side of the old beams if the damage is not too extensive. Regardless, your floor needs a lot of work. I thought we'd barricade the area for now. We should start on smaller, less costly repairs."

"Such as?"

"Such as replacing the broken window. Hanging the shutters. Stripping the dining room paneling. Scraping the exterior."

She nodded slowly, the fire in her hair warming his heart. "I agree in concept, but that gaping hole in my floor worries me."

Quentin finished the last sandwich. He needed to tread carefully here or Emma would balk. "Sometimes Stone Construction buys more supplies than it needs. I'll check the warehouse to see if there are excess materials we could use for the floor."

"That sounds great."

He gazed longingly at the intriguing woman beside him. He shouldn't push his luck any further tonight. He'd accomplished his goal of seeing her again. If he lingered here today, he might undo all of the ground he had won.

He rose to his feet. "Thanks for the sandwiches. It'll

be my turn to fix dinner tomorrow."

* * *

Ignoring the ringing phone, Emma spooned the last of the batter into the paper muffin cups. If she kept her eye on the time, she wouldn't ruin the muffin pan. After shoving it in the oven, she rinsed the thick mix off her fingers.

She answered her cell phone.

"Emma. It's Beverly."

A wave of guilt crested through Emma. She'd been too absorbed in Quentin to return Bev's call. She crossed the house to sit on the porch steps in the dusky twilight. "Bev. I meant to call you back. How are you?"

"I want to know what's going on out there. Don't sugar-coat it like you would for Maddy."

Emma's blood chilled. Did Beverly know about the floor collapse? Or that kiss? She hoped her secrets were safe. "Let's see. Right now I'm sitting on the porch while I bake a pan of blueberry muffins. Agnes jumped down from the bench to sit next to me."

"That's not what I mean. I'm talking about your plans to renovate the house."

She let out the breath she'd been holding. Her easy-going sister didn't know about the accident or the kiss, but she was spitting fire. Emma held her ground. "I'm going forward with the renovation."

"Renovating is a bad idea. A friend of mine helped repair a sink at his mother's house." Beverly's words came out fast. "The pipes were so old that he ended up having to replace all the plumbing. His mother took out a second loan to pay for everything. If you're that unhappy with your job, why don't you find a bed and breakfast to work at? Then you could move back to the city. We could all be close again."

This was her choice for a future. Why couldn't her sisters accept her decision? "You're missing the point, Bev. I don't want to work for anyone else. I want to be my own boss. This place would be a perfect retreat for city-weary folks."

Her sister inhaled sharply. "But, Em, even if you get the place spiffed up, you'll never get out of debt. It'll cost you a fortune."

"I'm not worried. I have good instincts when it comes to business. Trust me; I know what I'm doing. Besides, a friend is helping me." The moment the words left her mouth she knew she'd revealed too much.

Beverly wasn't a Heartly for nothing. "What friend?"

"I have friends. Are you implying I don't have any friends?" Emma winced at the sharp tone of her voice, wishing she sounded calmer.

"Of course not. Is it that Joel from your work?"

"What makes you think it's a man?"

"I'm not stupid. If it was a woman, you would have already told me her name."

A symphony of crickets chirped in the darkness shrouding the porch. Emma was glad for the immunity of night. If she pretended there was nothing to her friendship with Quentin, Beverly wouldn't know she melted inside at the sound of his voice or that she hoped he might end her long dry spell of abstinence. "His name is Quentin Stone. He knows a lot about this sort of thing."

"Quentin Stone? Of Stone Construction?"

"Yes."

"He volunteered to help you?"

Emma didn't enjoy being in the hot-seat. Agnes nosed her way under her palm. She drew strength from the touch. "Yes."

"When did you start dating him?"

"We're not dating," she huffed. The memory of that brief kiss flitted through her mind. She ruthlessly banished it. "He's a friend, that's all."

Laughter filled her ears. She waited in aggravated silence until Beverly could speak again.

"Do you want me to sign this Quit Claim Deed or not? If I sign it, your friend might not be around so much. I'd hate to be the reason you two parted company."

She drew in a quick breath. "You mean it? You'll sign?"

"Yes."

Her joyful whoop startled the crickets into silence. "Thank you, thank you. What made you change your mind?"

"You got me to thinking. You allowed us the opportunity to do what we wanted. If you don't want a career in science, you deserve a shot at something you do want. It's your turn."

"I'm speechless. My baby sister is growing up." Her heart swelled with pride. Her mind whirred with possibilities at the thought of getting a loan. One obstacle remained in her path: Maddy.

Beverly apparently shared the same thought. "One down, and one to go."

She scratched behind Agnes' ears thoughtfully. "I can't tell you how much it means to know you believe in me."

"Are you kidding? I've always believed in you. I spent my life trying to live up to your high expectations, so I know that this bed and breakfast idea of yours will turn out splendid. I'm sorry you doubted me. I wanted to protect you. Once I thought about it, putting constraints on my support was childish. I'll always love you, Em. You're my sister."

"Thanks, Bev."

She clicked off the phone. A light breeze from the lake stirred the air around her, cooling her body. Her future glimmered on the horizon. If only Maddy would cooperate. Secure in her newfound confidence, Emma punched up Maddy's home number on speed dial.

Maddy didn't answer. Probably out with her friends. She spoke to her sister's answering machine. "This is Emma. I hoped to talk to you, Maddy—"

"Em?"

"Hey. Are you having an early evening?"

"You could say that. Is something wrong?"

If she convinced Maddy to sign the Quit Claim Deed, she could fill out the loan papers tomorrow. She might even get the floor repaired before her sisters learned about the accident. "Why do you ask?"

"Because you never call me unless something is wrong or you need something."

She needed something all right. Her sister's cooperation. "Beverly phoned to tell me she would sign the Quit Claim Deed. I hoped you had time to reconsider too."

"I haven't changed my mind."

"Oh." She heard a male voice murmur something to Maddy. "Is this a bad time?"

"I have a friend over. Look, I don't want the place changed. I might want to spend an afternoon there sometime, and I want it to look like it always has."

"This place needs to be fixed up. It won't be here in a few years if something isn't done."

Maddy didn't respond, and Emma's hopes faded. Her sister's wall of stubbornness would block her plans unless she dismantled it. She needed to enlist Maddy's sympathy, and the best way to do that was to tell her about the accident.

She swallowed around the lump in her throat. "I didn't want to worry you with this, but you leave me no choice. When my friend Lucy and I removed the water-damaged boards in the living room, the entire floor caved in. This place needs help. Now. Not in a few years."

"What? When? Why didn't you say anything? Were you hurt?"

Emma chose to answer the last question. "I hit my head when I fell through to the basement. The Emergency Room doctor said I had a mild concussion. Lucy sprained her ankle."

"Oh, dear. I had no idea. I don't know what to say."

"Say you'll sign the deed. I need a loan to make repairs so this place can be safe."

"Come live with me. I have an extra bedroom. I don't want you taking chances with your life."

"You're missing the big picture. I'm not moving back to town. This is where I want to be, this is where I belong."

Her sister sniffed. "I'll think about it."

"Don't think too long. This place needs a lot of work."

Maddy's voice hardened. "You've made your point. Good night."

Her sister's abruptness didn't worry Emma. She was making headway. Maddy was considering the rehab.

Definite progress.

Her dog rolled over, exposing her underbelly. She gazed at Emma with pure, undisguised longing. She indulged her dog, rejoicing in her good fortune. Beverly believed in her. Once Maddy cooled down, she should come around. Heartly Inn would become a reality. And she'd be free of Joel. Hallelujah.

She stretched in contentment. The future yawned invitingly, sparkling with potential. She'd keep her focus on her goal of viable self-employment, no doubt about that, but along the way, she'd enjoy Quentin's helping hands.

Those wonderful hands.

She sighed dreamily, bringing in a deep breath of air. The rich smell of baking fruit caught her off guard. Her mouth watered at the intoxicating aroma. Her brain quickly connected the dots. The muffins! She scrambled to her feet.

Moments later, she removed a pan of well-done muffins from the oven. The burnt tops sliced right off. She popped one of the shaved muffins in her mouth. Not bad. With a little practice, she'd get the hang of this cooking thing.

The Heartly Inn would become her reality.

* * *

"Peach Melba. Ummm." Jeanie sighed blissfully. "Quentin, would your special restaurant cater my wedding?"

"No." Quentin wasn't about to cook for two hundred people on Jeanie's wedding day. He had enough to worry about with walking her down the aisle. And he planned to celebrate her marriage along with everyone else. He wouldn't have time for cooking. "They're strictly interested in staying small. Besides, you already have a caterer."

Jeanie licked her plate clean. "I do, but this is so yummy I'm thinking who needs wedding cake? Let's have Peach Melba instead."

"Jeanie, you will not change one thing about the wedding. The menu is set. Help me, Harrison," Dottie said.

Harrison grinned at his mother-in-law-to-be. "The only change I'm likely to approve is one that makes the wedding sooner than two weeks from now."

Jeanie flushed. "We can't change the date. There are too many people involved to change anything."

Harrison kissed Jeanie's hand. "Looks like we're right on track then."

John pushed back from the table with a groan. "This is getting out of hand. Before you know it, this table will be full of lovebirds."

Lucy's head popped up. She shot John an appraising glance. "What's going on?"

John nodded towards Quentin. "That's a good question. Quent, how are things with your new lady? When do we meet her?"

The delicious taste of the pie turned to dirt. Emma couldn't come to dinner until he was sure of her. The only thing he was sure of right now was that he was crazy about her. "You met her at the Emergency Room. What more do you want?"

Tabby giggled. "Details. We want details. Is she nice?"

Dottie's cherry-red scarf fell over her shoulder as she

collected the dessert plates. "Of course she's nice. Quentin wouldn't date someone who was mean."

"He's never home in the evenings. I've been by his place twice this week. He's never home," Alf volunteered.

John nodded. "Sounds serious all right. When is she coming to Sunday dinner?"

Quentin raised his hands in protest. "I'm building a friendship with Emma. That's all."

"A friendship?" Lucy repeated. "I saw the way you looked at her. That look went way beyond friendship. Emma and I are friends, but I don't look at her like she's Peach Melba."

"Can you blame me for taking it slow with Emma?" he asked. "I have a lousy track record with women. I don't need any family pressure."

John tossed him a lifeline. "Why don't you ply her with carryout from your favorite restaurant? That should win her over quicker than your manly charm, big brother."

Dottie slid back into her seat with a chuckle. "You said that old saying wrong, John. The quickest way to a man's heart is through his stomach. Women are different creatures entirely. They require romance, flowers, and jewelry."

John eyed the empty pie plate wistfully. "Too bad. I'd marry you, Quentin, if you fed me like this every day."

The dinner conversation flowed on to another topic, but Quentin's thoughts remained centered on Emma. The more time he spent with her, the more time he wanted from her. He wanted to hold her in his arms. He wanted to kiss her again.

A real kiss this time, one that set both of them on fire.

Soon, he promised himself.

Very soon.

CHAPTER SEVEN

Four evenings later, Emma knocked the dark goop off her paint scraper into a pail. She hugged a smile close to her heart as she worked. Quentin didn't have to be here helping, but he'd arrived as promised.

"How did you know this paneling would lighten up so much?" she asked, wonder laced through her voice. "This room has been a black hole forever."

"It might have been my years of experience in the house restoration industry." Quentin flashed a grin at her from across the dining room. "I am a highly skilled professional, you know."

She rocked back on her heels and inhaled the surprisingly pleasant citrus-scented wood stripping solvent. They'd done a wall a night. She glanced at the three completed walls, aware that her blood raced at the merest sound of his voice. "What was my great grandma thinking when she made this room so dark?"

"Everyone has a different decorating style. Maybe she had little lacey toppers on the furniture to lighten the room. My grandmother had a lot of those."

She shrugged and scraped more. "Still, this is incredible. I can't thank you enough for freeing me from the bat cave. I go to sleep at night with a big smile on my face because I know this room will be fabulous. People will marvel at these walls. They will be able to see what they're eating. Amazing."

"Speaking of eating, I should check on our dinner." Quentin carefully placed his paint scraper down on the drop cloth.

She wasn't planning to stare as he stretched his arms above his head. His actions riveted her. The sudden warmth infusing her body had her averting her eyes. She leapt to her feet. "Let me. It's the least I can do. I'm still savoring the leftovers from the last meal you brought out here." She called from the kitchen, "What was the name of that restaurant?"

"I didn't say," he replied. "If I told anyone where these meals come from, the chef would be overrun with business. Before you know it, he'd be too busy to accommodate me."

The meal was lukewarm, unlike Emma, who was roasting. She raised the oven temperature and strolled to the dining room.

Outside the open windows, bullfrogs and doves heralded the onset of twilight. A pleasant homey feeling infused her. Part of that ease came from working with Quentin.

She stood in the doorway watching him. He maneuvered the ladder to a new position, climbed it, and began scraping again. Quite unlike her variously speckled cutoffs and T-shirt, his pressed trousers and crisp white polo were immaculate. Every glob he'd scraped from the wall had made it to the disposal bucket. Good thing he did the high work, or she would have dripped black goop all over him.

With reluctance, she tore her gaze from his precise motions. She powered her scraper through the loosened gunk. "Dinner isn't ready yet. Remind me to check the oven soon because I turned the heat up."

He nodded. A few minutes later, he asked, "What do you do for fun?"

"Fun?" She choked on the foreign word. "What is fun? I've been meaning to ask someone the meaning of that word."

She dumped another batch of gunk into the bucket, spilling a bit on the drop cloth. Out of the corner of her eye, she noted a cat stalking the edge of the drop cloth where the fan lifted it from the floor. She could have sworn she'd put the cats outside before Quentin arrived this evening. Her heart rate kicked up.

"Shoo, Zelda. Don't come in here."

"Fun. Recreation. Leisure time," he continued. "You know, the activities you do in your spare time."

Like being in his arms? Like him kissing her again?

Romance wasn't on her schedule. She'd tried it and had been burned. She'd learned from her mistake. Her future was the Heartly Inn. She couldn't afford any distractions.

"Spare time?" She frowned. "You mean the time I'm not working on something?" She shook her head. "There's no such thing in my life."

"Don't you play tennis, rollerblade, country line dance, powerwalk, or another activity to keep fit?"

His line of inquiry ruffled her nerves. She didn't work out. So what? Not everyone had fitness fever. "Are you implying I'm fat?"

"Not at all," he answered smoothly. "I'm getting around to asking if you'd come with me to the driving range sometime. Golf is what I do for fun. There's nothing better than watching a little white ball sail off of the tee box."

Her scraper bogged down in the gunk. Was he asking her out? Better not go there. "Golf, eh? Never tried it. Thanks, but no thanks."

"Where's your sense of adventure?" His deep voice roughened. "Don't you want to know what fun is all about?"

She stopped to stare at him, aware he was talking about more than generic fun here. She needed to take charge of this conversation. "Hey, I'm not against having fun, but my priorities revolve around this place at the moment. Fixing this place up requires all of my energy. Not to mention my time and money."

His intensity lessened. "I hear you, but it's a mistake to always work. Are you afraid to spend non-working time with me?"

Zelda made a mad dash across the room, skittering through the piles of debris on the floor. Grateful for the distraction, Emma focused her aggravation on the frenetic cat, stomping her bare feet loudly, wishing she were as focused as she claimed. Right now, a certain contractor was a huge distraction. "Git. Zelda. Shoo!"

After a moment, Quentin prompted her. "You didn't answer me."

Her cheek twitched. Their relationship was platonic, and that was for the best. She didn't need a man in her life. She didn't want one either. Not after the way Joel had broken her heart. She didn't ever want to feel that bad again.

He wasn't Joel. For one, he helped her. He followed through on his promises. His patience seemed inexhaustible. He had the sexiest voice on the planet. If she wanted a boyfriend, Quentin would be her first choice.

The family motto sprang to mind. Heartlys didn't date handsome men. She didn't need a broken heart while she changed careers. She preferred their current arrangement. "You're a decent guy. A great friend. And I hope you don't take this the wrong way. This is as far as I want to go with our friendship."

His fingers stroked the length of his paint scraper. "You agree we're good friends?"

She nodded, pleased his taut features had relaxed. "Yes." Not many people would volunteer to help with a big project like this.

"Friends do stuff together," he reminded her.

Too late, she realized the snare he'd set for her. "Yes, but—"

He forestalled the rest of her protest with a curt wave of his hand. "No excuses. We're friends. Friends do stuff together."

"Oh, all right," she grumbled. She'd worry about her resolve and self-control later. "We're friends. You've made your point. Someday I'll go golfing with you."

He beamed his approval. "Now that we've straightened that out, what about dinner?"

"Dinner!" She scrambled out of the room, grateful for the reprieve. If she'd burned his delicious smelling meal, she would cry.

If only she could find a chef of this quality, her B&B would be on the map in no time. Not that she could afford to pay his secret chef. She sighed with regret.

She delivered the plates of food to the table, mentally reviewing their conversation. Had she agreed to date him?

A handsome man like Quentin probably had gorgeous women falling all over him. His interest flattered her, but how would he feel tomorrow? Or the next day? Once someone else happened along, he would forget all about her.

Depressing.

Thank God she had this perfect meal to comfort her tonight. She hummed in delight over the moist Cornish game hen. "This is yummy. Thanks for bringing dinner."

"My pleasure. Picking up the food in town gives us more time to focus on the rehab."

He filled the breakfast nook with his presence, and her thoughts turned unprofessional once again. Would he touch her tonight? She'd been thinking of how wonderful it would be to feel the weight of his hands. Silly imaginings, especially when she shouldn't encourage his interest.

Did she give off mixed signals? If his goal was romance, and hers was home repair, one of them would be disappointed. It would be best if she cleared the air.

"I feel like I'm taking advantage of you," she began. "This is so wonderful, having you help me with the house. I enjoy these great meals you bring out."

His brown eyes warmed. "It's my pleasure to be here. I enjoy your company."

"But not my cooking?" she teased.

"There's a lot to be said for a good peanut butter sandwich. You make the best ones I've ever eaten."

His voice rumbled through her, filling the emptiness

inside. Was she a challenge to him? As she worried, headlights reflected off the window. A car approached.

"Are you expecting anyone?" He peered through the living room screen door.

She ducked in front him to see. Mere inches separated them, and the heat from his body warmed her. She shivered with awareness. "I'm not expecting anyone."

Her warbling voice caused her to cringe inwardly. Why did she feel guilty about his presence? They weren't doing anything wrong. Quentin was a friend.

His hand rested heavily on her shoulder, fueling her secret longings, stirring her emotions. She allowed herself a moment to revel in the sensations, to pretend they were a couple. A second later, guilt rushed in. She couldn't have it both ways.

"I'll get rid of whoever it is, if you like," he offered, his low voice buzzing in her ear.

She squinted into the darkness. From the shape of the headlights, she knew who'd come for a visit. Her jaw clenched. "It's my sister."

"Do you want me to leave?"

She shot him a questioning glance over her shoulder. "No way. Two heads are better than one when it comes to managing Maddy. I should warn you, she's a whirlwind."

"I'm not afraid of a little wind."

She leaned close to his ear. "Don't say I didn't warn you."

"If it isn't Ma and Pa Kettle." Maddy bounced up the stairs. Her figure-flattering white suit glowed in the dark. "Who is this delicious chunk of manhood, Sis?"

"Quentin is a friend." Her sister couldn't have picked a worse time to intrude. All day long she looked forward to this time with Quentin. With a sigh, she made the introductions. "He's helping me with the renovation."

Maddy extended her hand to him, waggling her fingers. "Uh-huh. You two look quite cozy. Why didn't you tell me you were dating such a handsome man?"

To her chagrin, he took forever shaking her sister's hand. He wasn't hers, but she didn't want him to be Maddy's either.

Before she could get a word out, Quentin answered for her. "I'm delighted to meet Emma's sister. You're a beautiful woman, Maddy, but I'm sure you hear that every day."

Maddy's tinkling laughter grated on Emma's nerves. One of her sister's hands captured his arm. "There's hearing it, and there's *hearing* it. Coming from you, I take it as *quite* a compliment."

She glanced down at her paint-speckled clothes. She didn't hold a candle to her sister's sleek style or witty repartee. Male attention spans were fleeting, but she'd hoped for a little more time with Quentin. Maddy's arrival changed things. He seemed to be thoroughly enjoying her sister's fawning.

Emma wasn't.

Not that she ever enjoyed flirting. She preferred talking in a straightforward manner about real topics. Talking about compliments was a waste of time.

Her stomach twisted into a knot. She didn't have any right to be upset at his warm reaction to her sister's flirting. He enjoyed female attention. He was a free agent. End of story.

Who was she kidding? She was upset. Jealous, too. And aggravated about the situation. Her sister's rapt masculine adoration sickened her. She wanted to bat

Maddy's hand off his broad chest.

"What do you want, Maddy?" she asked.

"I do believe Emma is a little jealous," Maddy purred.

She started to deny that claim, but realized she would be playing right into her sister's hands if she protested. No one played games better than her sister. "I've worked two jobs today. I'm too tired to play games. Did you change your mind about deeding the property over to me?"

"Who wants to talk about that boring deed when you've got such fascinating company? I insist Quentin give me the tour from a contracting perspective."

Her anger ratcheted up another notch at Maddy's casual dismissal of the all-important house deed. "Could you think about someone besides yourself for a change? You don't need a tour of the house you grew up in."

"Yes. I do. I need to see this place through Quentin's contractor eyes."

She raised her hands in mock surrender. "Suit yourself. I've got work to do."

"I always suit myself."

As her sister's easy banter echoed throughout the house, Emma felt sick to her stomach. She sealed up the disposal pail and carried the scrapers to the laundry room to wash, her footfalls heavy on the floor. If only she could seal up her thoughts so easily. Men never looked at her when her sister was around. She became a wallflower.

Her foray into romance had been a disaster. Joel had walked all over her. It was probably good that she had this wake-up call with Quentin. She'd suspected he'd lose interest in the future, but she'd never expected he'd drift away so soon.

Why did it have to be Maddy who took him away? One would think her sister would sense Quentin's importance to her, that her sister wouldn't flirt with him right in front of her. One might think that if her sister wasn't Maddy.

She sighed.

Hiding in the laundry room wouldn't work long-term. If he preferred her sister, she'd face that disappointment head-on.

She joined them in the dining room, and they startled apart. It appeared they'd been telling secrets, or at least discussing something private. Her cheeks burned.

Had they been laughing at her naivete with men? Her gaze narrowed. Just because she chose not to waste time flirting didn't mean she couldn't do it. Quentin had probably asked her sister out, and Maddy had probably said yes.

Her shoulders slumped.

Quentin checked his watch. "Look at the time. I've got to get going."

"Me too," Maddy said. "I'll walk you out."

As they left, Emma's hands clenched together. Usually after supper, they sat on the steps for a bit. Not tonight, though. He'd taken one look at her sexy sister, and he couldn't get away from Emma fast enough.

She sat down on the weathered steps with Agnes. She stroked her dog's head mindlessly, grateful for the company. The sharp ache in her heart surprised her. Why did it matter that Quentin and Maddy got along famously? Why did it matter that he hadn't spoken to her once her sister arrived?

She didn't know why, but it mattered. A lot. She

hadn't forgotten the wonderful sensations she'd experienced in Quentin's arms the day her floor broke. Or that poignant kiss that had awakened her. He'd been nothing but attentive to her since.

Until tonight.

With another sigh, she stroked Agnes' soft ears. She wasn't fooling herself. Not for a red hot minute. She had feelings for the man that stretched beyond friendship. How could she watch Quentin fall for Maddy? Her sister collected handsome men the way other women collected shoes or purses. Maddy kept a man until someone new came along, then she upgraded to a different model. Men were the accessories of her life.

She couldn't bear for Quentin to be treated like excess footwear. He was too nice for such callous treatment. He deserved someone who thought he was special, someone who wouldn't consider him disposable.

Someone like…Emma.

* * *

Quentin pulled over at the head of the graveled lane, exited his Jeep, and stood near his headlights. He wasn't keen on meeting Emma's overbearing sister alone, but he couldn't refuse. From the way she'd flirted with him, he was half-afraid she would ask for his number.

A lump formed in his stomach.

Maddy was a beautiful, passionate woman, the kind he used to seek out, but after Emma's genuine warmth, Maddy's artificial flash held no allure. He preferred truthful, straightforward women who knew what they wanted. Maddy was complicated. He didn't do complicated anymore.

Maddy hurried through the darkness to his side. "What's the deal with you and my sister?"

Ah, so it was *that* kind of a talk. He hadn't had to justify his intentions since high school prom. The lump in his throat tightened. "She already explained the deal. We're friends."

"I'm not stupid." Fire blazed in her eyes. "The vibe I picked up in that house was strong. Are you sleeping with her?"

Her anger seemed out of proportion when one considered that Emma was a grown woman. "No. We're friends. I enjoy Emma's company, and I love working on old houses."

"Are you using my sister? I won't have it. You don't want to cross me about Emma. She got steamrollered by another loser."

His eyes narrowed in anger. "I know about Joel."

Her brows shot up. "She told you about him?"

"Yeah. I offered to beat him up for her."

"How primitive. I love it." Maddy tapped her fingernails on her crossed arms. "She isn't strong enough to fend off another seduction. My sister is emotionally fragile."

He planned to take care of Emma. He wanted to protect her from the hard knocks of life. She needed him to look out for her. "I know that."

"If she allows you to hang around, why haven't you pushed for more than friendship?"

"She's not the only one with a history. My luck with women is lousy. I want to get this right. Emma's too special to rush into anything."

"You seem like a guy who moves fast."

She'd gotten his number. Interesting. "That would be

the old me. The one with four failed engagements."

Maddy rocked back on her heels. "Wow. That is lousy luck. What's wrong with you?"

"Not a thing."

She smirked. "Yeah. I bet you're perfect. Such a great catch four other women threw you back. Seriously, what's the deal?"

"Seriously, I'm perfect. Except for being goal-oriented. I accomplish what I set out to accomplish. Only with Emma, I plan to hang on this time."

"Goal-oriented." She made a tsking sound. "Sounds like stubborn to me. You might be good for each other. But I have to warn you, if you hurt her, I'll hunt you down. The Heartly girls stick together."

She rose in his estimation. "Family is important. I wouldn't have it any other way."

Maddy nodded back towards the house. "You really think that old place can be turned into a viable business?"

"Sure do."

"She can't cook. Serving breakfast is integral to running a B&B."

Her comment unnerved him. She couldn't possibly know about his cooking secret. He scrambled to re-orient himself. "You expect me to teach her how to cook?"

"Lord, no. That would be a miracle." A genuine smile brightened Maddy's made-up face. "Emma's avoided cooking all of her life. I'm expecting this B&B idea to blow over."

He didn't agree with her assessment. "Emma is determined to rehab the house. I don't see her changing her mind."

She jabbed her finger in his chest. "Be kind to my sister, or I will hurt you. You do not want to make me mad."

With that she roared off in her little white car. He didn't have any problem with her ultimatum. He'd treat Emma like spun glass. Would she return the favor?

* * *

A few days later, Emma fingered the snug fabric covering her breasts. She hardly recognized the sophisticated woman in Bev's bathroom mirror. The glamorous woman returning her gaze seemed capable of knocking a man off his feet. It was a shame to waste this outfit on a work function.

She'd love to strut by Quentin in this body-hugging dress. To see if he noticed how sexy she looked. "Thanks for helping me out on such short notice. I forgot to have my taupe suit cleaned after the last business dinner Joel ordered me to attend."

"You look better in my dress than I do." Bev lifted Emma's hair up off her shoulders. "You should dress up more often."

"I don't know about that. The dress fits, but I feel like I don't have room for a full breath or dinner."

Bev beamed into the mirror. "That's the beauty of the stretchy fabric. Eat all you want. The dress will expand."

"You don't think it's too, well, provocative, for a business dinner?"

"Nope. You can't go wrong in a little black dress. It's a fashion staple. This is the most conservative black dress in my closet."

"Dang. If this one's conservative, I'm glad you didn't expect me to wear the other ones."

"You look nice, Em. I guarantee you will be the hit of this business party." Bev gathered Emma's hair into a sleek knot. I'm thinking a French twist for your hair."

She admired the stylish effect. "You've got such an eye for this. Truthfully, I should wear a burlap sack because it's Joel's investment clients."

Bev mumbled around a mouthful of bobby pins. "If you didn't want to do it, why'd you agree to go?"

"He made it a condition of my continued employment."

"Stinker."

"Yeah. He thought I would forgive him for screwing Barb. He asked if he could pick me up tonight, like this was a date."

Alarm flared in Bev's dark eyes. "You're not thinking about dating him again are you?"

"Heck, no. He's blown his chance with me. I'll attend his business dinner, then I'm headed home. Alone. Thanks for sprucing me up Bev."

Bev held out a pair of strappy heels. "Here. Wear these."

Emma donned the shoes. She looked great. She'd do her job and get out of there. If she had time, she'd like to paint the dining room window trim tonight.

Quentin had cancelled on her last night. He was probably out with Maddy right now. Good thing she'd stuck to her guns about keeping the rehab her priority.

* * *

Quentin's blood ran cold and hot. His flashlight did little to cut the relative gloom of Emma's basement or the gathering storm clouds in his mind. The fresh saw marks on the floor joists spiked his blood pressure.

Methodically, he ran the beam of the light over the joists near the gaping hole. Each beam had blunt ends. None were ragged as expected in an accidental break.

One joint might have snapped clean in two. Not all of them. Something was very wrong here.

Was Emma handy enough with tools to have ruined her own floor? He shook that thought away immediately. He'd worked beside the woman for days now. This place was her passion. She wouldn't sabotage something she wanted so much, something she worked so hard to repair.

These cuts were deliberate.

Someone wanted the floor to fail.

Someone who didn't care who got hurt.

His pulse thundered in his ears. Who would want such a thing?

Her sisters had been against the renovation at first. Then Emma's youngest sister had changed her mind. Maddy would soon change hers. The look on Maddy's face as he'd told her of Emma's fall revealed a lot about Maddy's state of mind. No, Emma's sisters weren't behind this.

Who could it be?

More to the point, how could he keep Emma safe?

He ascended the basement steps with a heavy heart. Things were at a precarious point between him and Emma. If he came down hard on her about personal security, he might spook her.

Since the night Maddy had visited, Emma had been distant. Her icy reserve bothered him.

He'd broken down and purchased flowers for Emma yesterday, but his sister's car broke down at the mall. It had taken all three Stone brothers to get the car running again. By then it had been too late to come out to Emma's. He'd cancelled and offered the flowers to his sister.

Glancing at his watch again, he wished she'd notified him about her delay. Two hours late. Where was she?

Was she with another man?

He wanted her in his arms, in his bed. He couldn't stop thinking about her insistence that they were only friends. Could there be another man in her life?

He sure as hell hoped not.

When he'd arrived this evening, he'd been caught off guard by her absence. He'd sat on the porch with her pets, waiting for her to come home. He'd decided to surprise her by getting a head start on the evening's work. The house was open, as usual. He'd placed a covered skillet of beef stroganoff in her oven and began cleaning up the basement below the living room.

That's when he'd made his chilling discovery.

He couldn't work on anything. All he could do was wait. He poured himself a glass of freshly brewed iced tea and sat down on the porch. If she didn't come soon, he would call her sisters.

Dusk fell before her headlights appeared in the lane. He dumped the kittens from his lap and stood. He concentrated on staying calm. Not easy when he was overwrought about her safety.

Emma stepped from the car in a slinky black number that accentuated every curve on her body. Her sleekly twisted hair enhanced her natural elegance. High heels dangled from her hands, drawing his gaze down shapely calves to her incredibly sexy feet. In an outfit like that, she'd been dining on champagne and caviar. Most likely with another man.

Her face glowed. It tore him up that someone else was responsible for her happy expression. He wanted her to light up like that for him. He wanted all of her smiles and tender touches.

Had she gone out to dinner with another man?

He didn't have the right to feel betrayed, but there it was. A lousy feeling infecting him like the flu. He wanted to hurl his glass of tea against the side of the house, only what would that solve? Instead, he rammed his curled fists into his pockets.

As she approached, a curious cocktail of emotions overtook the last vestige of his common sense. Anger swirled around frustration. He ached with wanting to kiss her again. She was so sweetly beautiful. How much longer could he go on being her friend when he craved more from her?

He took a deep breath. His plan was to politely inquire why she was late. But he should have remembered basic meteorology because as he opened his mouth to speak, pure lightning surged out of it. "Where the hell have you been?"

CHAPTER EIGHT

He came.

Emma hurried toward the man who haunted her dreams. After Quentin had begged off last night, she'd been unsure of his presence this evening. She'd been afraid it would be presumptuous to contact him telling him her plans for the night had changed.

Even more afraid he'd been with another woman last night.

But he was here.

Euphoria bubbled through her, happily dancing over every nerve ending. She'd nursed one glass of white wine the entire evening, but that hadn't caused her giddiness. Quentin had. She hadn't lost him to another woman.

He was here.

On her porch.

The thick perfume of twilight honeysuckle swirled around her. Everything was once again right in her world. The boring business dinner she'd been compelled to attend faded from memory. Quentin's presence on her porch filled her with joy.

Breathlessly, she skipped up the porch stairs. Would he notice her dress? It had brought her plenty of masculine attention all evening. She wanted him to respond in that way, too. She wanted to take his breath away, same as he took hers away.

But he'd yelled at her for being late.

She stilled. "What's wrong?"

He glared at her. "You left your house unlocked. You're too trusting. There are saw marks on your floor joists. Saw marks! Now do you understand why you have to lock the doors?"

She shook her head to see if the underwater sensation she felt would abate. His fury disoriented her. She hadn't done anything wrong. He paused for a breath, and she put a hand on his arm. Sparks shot up her arm, adding to her mental confusion. "I don't understand. Calm down. Start over."

He leaned toward her face. "I won't be calm for a very long time. Do you have any enemies?"

"Enemies?" her heart raced. "What are you talking about?"

With her hand tucked in his, he marched her through the house. "I want you to see something."

Energy pulsed through their linked fingers. In spite of Quentin's foul mood, his touch felt right. Warmth coursed through her.

She knew better than to hope for more than friendship with him. Maddy was his type. But she couldn't turn the wanting off. Why couldn't he see her as a woman?

She ached for him.

Not good.

Not good at all.

She was in serious trouble here.

She descended the basement stairs. How did Maddy do it? How did Maddy keep her heart whole as she rotated men through her life?

His flashlight sliced through the considerable gloom of the musty basement. He'd been working in her absence. The thought cheered her. Ruined furniture and broken floorboards had been stacked in a neat pile near the stairs. "You've been busy."

Tension vibrated through his hand as he aimed the light toward the hole in the ceiling. "Look."

The hole looked tidy, the wood edges smooth. Nothing here to justify his over-the-top distress. "You sawed all the joist ends? Thanks, now we can do that sistering thing you mentioned with the beams."

He stilled. "I didn't touch the joists."

The chill in his voice stopped her. She couldn't catch her breath. "What do you mean?"

"Your fall was no accident. These boards were cut. Deliberately."

She blinked slowly, trying to get her bearings in this mental quicksand. "Why would anyone cut the boards?"

"Why indeed?"

Her heart thumped wildly. Her expensive lobster appetizer cartwheeled through her stomach. She exhaled slowly to steady her nerves.

Someone had trespassed in her house. They had damaged the floor beams. Why? Who hated her so much?

A tremor snaked down her spine. She stared up at the hole again. Someone had deliberately cut the boards. Someone wanted to hurt her. She couldn't get past those facts. They circled her head like a toy train on a track.

The anger he telegraphed to her tightened the knot in her stomach. She knew he wanted her to say something, but she had no words for the horror she felt. "I don't understand any of this."

"You can't think of anyone who has it in for you?"

She shook her head in a rapid motion. "I can't believe someone came out here. That they were in my house."

"Your security has to be upgraded. This can't happen again."

Thoughts collided in her head. She had an enemy? Who? How? Why? It seemed too bizarre to be true. Quentin steered her out of the basement and into the kitchen. She tried to get a grip on her disorientation.

It didn't work.

She had the sinking feeling her life would never be the same again. In a daze, she allowed him to seat her at the breakfast nook. Who hated her? Hate was such a strong emotion. Surely, she'd know if someone hated her. She began running through a mental list of acquaintances.

"You want that?" he asked.

She glanced down at her full plate. "Help yourself."

While the situation had sapped her appetite, it seemed to have had the reverse effect on him. "I'll be moving in here until we get this sorted out," he announced.

She blinked in surprise. "What?"

His gaze connected with hers, scalding her with its intensity. Her lower lip trembled. This whole lets-be-friends plan wasn't working. She needed a good hug, and she wanted him to offer it right now.

As if he'd read her mind, he opened his arms to her. She hopped on his lap, savoring his strength.

His unique woodsy fragrance filled her heart with contentment. She sighed. Fear had prompted her action, but she'd desired this for the longest time. This was where she wanted to be.

He nuzzled her ear, kissed her neck. "Sweetheart, I'm sorry if I frightened you. Truth is, I had a pretty big fright myself when I found the saw marks. Then you were late. I worried something else might have gone wrong. I want you to be safe. That's why I'm staying out here until we get to the bottom of this."

She struggled to think. With her insides twisted in knots, nothing made sense. He'd called her sweetheart. Did he call all women that, or was it a special endearment for her alone?

She replayed his last words. He was staying here? "I can take care of myself."

He stroked her hair. "Yes, you can, but I'm going to help you. We'll install new locks on your doors and windows. We'll get to the bottom of this. I promise."

She surged to her feet. "I'm not a wimp."

"Your safety is in jeopardy. We both had a scare tonight. Let me protect you, that's all I'm asking. Otherwise, I'll worry myself sick."

"You believe someone wants to hurt me?"

"I do, yes."

"You're not saying that to sleep under my roof?"

"No."

"Because I'm worried about the other."

"The other?"

"I just ended a bad relationship. I'm worried about our friendship, worried about my resolve weakening, worried about my B&B derailing."

"I'm not following you, Red."

She glared at him. "You're distracting me, you dolt. I can't concentrate. You hugged me. You kissed my neck. No wonder I'm flustered."

He grinned at her. "That's a good thing."

"It's bad, I tell you. I can't manage extra pressure right now. I'm on the cusp of changing careers. I can't deal with the added time constraints of building a relationship. I need a friend more than a boyfriend."

"Let's compromise. I'll see to your safety. You set the pace for our friendship. Agreed?"

She didn't want to accept anyone's help. She needed to maintain her independence, to show the world that Heartly women didn't crack under pressure. But she'd never dealt with a threat to her personal safety. Why hadn't she taken self-defense classes?

Quentin made her feel safe. Why was she hesitating? She wasn't a coward, but she wasn't stupid either. She nodded. "Agreed."

He whisked her off to bed, waiting outside the bathroom while she changed clothes and brushed her teeth. He tucked her in and turned to leave.

Before he closed the door, he whispered, "Nice dress."

A big smile spread across Emma's face. He'd noticed.

She wasn't a totally sexless, incompetent female. Whatever this relationship was, she liked it more with each passing moment.

* * *

The next few days passed in a blur of activity for Emma. Quentin insisted that every exterior door have a keyed deadbolt and that every window have a lock. With reluctance, she wrote out a large check for the locksmith. That money would have paid for many building supplies. At this rate, she'd have to save like crazy to have anything to put toward supplies.

When Lucy learned what had happened, she offered to keep her company for the weekend. Emma turned her down flat. "No way. I don't want you getting hurt again. This is my problem. I'll get through it."

"Someone should stay with you, or you should relocate." Lucy thumped her crutches on the tile laboratory floor to emphasize her point. "If a crazy person is after you, you're isolated at the lake. Why don't you move in with me or your sisters?"

"This is embarrassing to admit, but your brother felt the same way. He's moved in with me until this is over." Heat radiated from her face in waves. "But he didn't move-in-with-me move in, he's staying at my place. With me. But not with me, if you know what I mean."

The tension receded from Lucy's face. "Quentin's staying there? Why didn't you say so? I'll see you at Sunday dinner?"

"Sunday dinner?" she repeated slowly.

"Our family gets together every week for a family meal. Isn't he bringing you this Sunday?"

She died a little inside. Friends did things together. He'd been clear about that point. "He hasn't mentioned it."

"Let's surprise him. Come as my guest. The desserts Quentin brings are divine."

The idea of surprising him appealed to her. "Is it a Pot Luck then? Should I bring a dish?"

"No. You're company. Come and enjoy."

"All right." She finished signing the stack of sampling reports. "How are things in your life?"

Her friend sighed. "When you don't have a steady man in your life, every man you meet seems interesting. Have you ever noticed how Herb Goodlow's biceps fill out his sleeves? I'd like to get to know him better."

"Herb?" Emma shook her head dismissively. "Get a grip. He glares at me during every staff meeting. I've done nothing to make him mad."

Lucy chuckled. "You mean, other than run his department better than anyone else ever has? You have a flair for management. I bet your B&B will set new records in the hospitality industry."

"I can only hope. I'd hate to give up this cushy job on the cutting edge of science for nothing."

Her friend cleared her throat pointedly. "How are you getting along with Quentin?"

She remembered the argument they'd had over breakfast. She wasn't a morning person, but he'd insisted she eat the eggs he'd prepared. "Your brother is a tyrant. When he wants to make a point, he digs in. There's no changing his mind. He's driving me nuts."

Lucy folded over with laughter, rocking wildly on her crutches. Between laughs she managed to say, "You come to dinner at my Mom's on Sunday evening. I've got to see this."

She shook her head in wonderment. Lucy thought his bossiness was funny? It wasn't humorous to her, not one bit. He insisted she keep the house locked up tight. If poor Agnes didn't exit the house with them in the morning, she had to spend the day inside and she'd already had one doggie mishap. Gone were the days when Agnes could push the screen door open with her nose.

Quentin had taken charge of her life. Besides the house locks, he'd taken over the rehab. She wasn't sure when she lost the power struggle on that one. In the beginning, she selected what project they would do next. She may have asked him for a suggestion or two, but now, he decided everything. He decided on the quality of supplies he brought out to the house. He'd even decided what color to apply to her dining room paneling.

Of course, his choices were the ones she would have made. That was beside the point. He made decisions for her. It irked her to no end.

Not once on Friday or Saturday did he mention his Sunday dinner to her. Late Sunday morning, he'd handed her a long list of things to do. She studied the list. He'd put down enough chores to keep four people busy for a week.

"What's this?" she asked.

"I have to go into town for the afternoon. That's our status list, so you'll know which projects are safe to tackle in my absence."

Her voice sweetened like cane syrup. "Why thank you. That's so kind of you to make me a list."

He ignored her sarcasm and shouldered his bulging gym bag. "I'll be back a little after dark. Keep everything locked while I'm gone."

She'd planned to wash her laundry today. It would be no trouble to add his clothes. "I'll do those, if you like." She reached for his bag.

"No thanks. Jeanie takes care of my wash for me."

Emma saw red for a moment. Then she remembered Jeanie was his sister. She took a deep breath. "All right. See you later."

After he left, her footsteps echoed hollowly through the old house. He'd only been in residence for a few days but she'd come to rely on his company. His sexy smiles were as necessary as his gentle touches. In his absence, longing filled her, a longing to be near him every second of the day.

What was she going to do about this? Her physical attraction wasn't lessening as they spent more time together. It was intensifying. That in itself was a warning things were out of her control. Was he beginning to care for her? Or was he like Joel and wanted a convenient sexual partner?

After he'd discovered the cut boards, she'd been sure that Quentin cared for her as more than a friend. She'd tried to keep him at arm's length because she didn't trust her emotions, but he'd invaded her heart anyway.

Time to shake the man up a little bit.

Lucy had made her promise to arrive late for Sunday dinner. Emma wasn't much on grand entrances, but Quentin would recognize her car if she arrived on time. No point in spoiling the big surprise. She wanted to see how he reacted to being caught unawares, to having his honest reaction on display.

She surveyed her wardrobe. Too old. Too tight. Too brown. Too wrinkled. Too frumpy. She had nothing to wear, but she had the next best thing. A sister who was her size.

She called Beverly. "Clothing crisis. I need to look presentable yet casually chic."

Beverly's delighted laughter filled the airwaves. "Come on over. Am I fixing your hair too?"

Her hair? Would it seem like a date if she had her hair done? "Nothing fancy. My friend Lucy invited me to her family dinner, but I don't want to overdo it. And my work clothes remind me of how much I hate my job."

"Bring my little black dress and heels back when you come. How much time do I have to make you gorgeous?"

She glanced at her alarm clock. "Not long. Dinner is in two hours. It'll take me an hour to get to your place."

"Casually chic, right? I've got a great outfit."

"Thanks, Sis. You're the best."

* * *

The woman in the full-length mirror looked great. Beverly's linen sheath, slouchy teal jacket, and matching teal heels fit Emma to the letter.

"Where do you find clothes like these?" she asked.

Beverly's gaze darted to the door again. "I didn't find them. Maddy did, when she took me shopping for my birthday last year. I should warn you, she'll be here any minute."

Her heart sank, and her nerves spun into overdrive. "I wish you hadn't done that. Maddy made it clear that she hates the idea of me changing the house into a bed and breakfast. She's so stubborn."

"That she is." Beverly's voice softened. "But she had the best teacher in the world for assertiveness training. You."

She clutched her chest. "Me? You think I'm stubborn?"

"Yeah." Beverly nodded, the corners of her lips twitching. "You're pig-headed and obstinate, like Maddy. Luckily, I'm the perfect sister. I want you two to get along. That's why I invited her over here."

She shuddered. "I'd rather have a sharp stick poked

in my eye."

"See what I mean? You're stubborn."

A surge of adrenaline caused her words to tumble out unedited. "Hey, stubborn kept a roof over our heads as kids. Stubborn got us decent educations and a chance to make something of ourselves. You can't say stubborn is a bad thing."

"It has its place, but you can't solve every problem with a take-no-prisoners attitude. You have to learn to give and take."

Emma shook her head. "I disagree. You show weakness, and you get eaten for breakfast."

"We're not talking about the big bad world. We're talking about getting along with your sister."

"Even more reason not to show any weakness. Maddy goes for the jugular every time."

There was a knock at the door. "I'll get that," Beverly said. "I'm expecting you to play nice."

She wanted Maddy to sign off on the Quit Claim Deed. How could she compromise on that? It represented her future. Emma squared her shoulders for battle. "Hello, Maddy."

Her sister breezed in, armed with a bulging tote bag. "Hello, yourself. You look nice in Beverly's birthday outfit. Your boyfriend won't know what hit him."

Emma couldn't stop a frown from filling her face. "That's the problem. Quentin isn't my boyfriend. But I'd like to encourage his attention."

Maddy dropped her large tote on the bed. "I'd love to do your make-up."

She'd planned on dabbing on lip gloss and calling it good. It wasn't like Maddy to offer anything. "You would?"

"Yeah." Maddy leveled her gaze at Emma. "The artist in me wants to complete this pretty picture."

Her gaze darted from sister to sister. She didn't miss the encouraging smile Beverly shot her. Maddy was offering her an olive branch. She'd be a fool to refuse. "All right."

Maddy grabbed a bag of cosmetics from her tote. She motioned toward the door. "Let's do this in the kitchen. The natural lighting is better, plus there's room for all of us."

She sat at the table, completely at her sister's mercy. "Don't forget that I'm allergic to that waterproof mascara," she cautioned.

"I'm not likely to forget." Maddy's dramatic sigh filled the cozy kitchen. "Your eyelids plumped up like sausages last time. I brought along a hypoallergenic tube of the old-fashioned kind for you. Thanks for trusting me to do this."

She swiveled to glance up at Maddy. "Of course I trust you. We didn't know about the allergy last time you did my makeup. I never thought you were to blame."

Maddy held her gaze. "Good. I wouldn't do anything to hurt you."

Her sister had enough confidence to design entire office interiors, but she worried about Emma's opinion? Time for a little reassurance. "I know that."

"Okay. Stop talking so I can work my magic."

"See how nice this is," Beverly said a few minutes later. "My sisters are under the same roof. Better still, they are getting along. I do have a family."

A pang of guilt stabbed Emma's heart. She'd never meant for her dream to tear her family apart. "We'll always be family. Even when we disagree."

"About that disagreeing thing," Maddy started. Her voice trailed off.

Beverly prompted Maddy with a friendly shove. "I'm getting to it," Maddy grumbled.

"We have something for you." Beverly picked up a packet of papers on the counter. "Something we shouldn't have withheld from you. Our whole-hearted trust. You're our sister. We've always believed in you."

Emma's chest constricted. She couldn't bring herself to reach for the papers. "I don't know what to say."

Maddy took the papers from Beverly. She put them in front of Emma. "Say you'll forgive us. We were looking out for you. We didn't want you to be burdened with debt."

Tears welled up in her eyes. "You were looking out for me?" When had her sisters grown up? She'd thought they couldn't forget the past. Instead, they'd been thinking about the future. Her future.

"Yeah. You've always sacrificed for us." Maddy tucked the cosmetics back in the bag. "We're grateful for the things you've done. We wanted you to have your shot. It took us awhile to realize your shot came along because it wasn't what we wanted for you."

Stars danced in Beverly's eyes. "I wanted you to find a wonderful man and have a houseful of kids. You've been like a second Mom to us for years. You're a natural with kids, Em."

"I wanted you to never have to worry about money again," Maddy added. "I thought if you stayed in town you'd have a better chance at stumbling over a tycoon. There's no one out in the boonies who meets my affluent criteria for you."

Beverly squeezed Emma's hand. "Yeah, but you

want something different. Your heart is set on the B&B. We didn't have the right to insist on our future for you. We had the luxury of choice, something you never had."

Her sisters really *had* grown up. Emma fanned the heat from her face. She glanced down at the notarized Quit Claim Deed. "I'm speechless."

"About damn time," Maddy said. She pulled Emma to her feet for a hug. "Now don't you start crying or you'll ruin my makeup job."

"I never cry," Emma sniffed. "Thank you both so much. I won't let you down."

"No, you won't." Maddy laughed. "Because I will beat your butt if you do. Go on over to the Stones. See if you can't wrap that handsome man around your little finger. He's rich enough to suit me. I'll bet with all the family he's got, he's planning on a large brood of his own one day. The way I see it, you land him, we all get what we want."

She hugged her sisters again. "Thank you. From the bottom of my heart."

* * *

Emma parked her Saturn behind a white Toyota on the city street. The address Lucy had given her was in a quiet Baltimore neighborhood with immaculate lawns. The huge two-story house would make a perfect bed and breakfast, she mused.

With confidence, she strode to the door and rang the bell. Quentin would be so thrilled that she could afford to hire his company now. She couldn't wait to tell him the good news.

A brawny fellow with Quentin's chin opened the

door. He swooped her into a big bear hug. "You're my birthday present, right?"

She shrieked in alarm. "Put me down. I'm Emma Heartly, Lucy's friend. I'm expected."

His luminous brown eyes twinkled at her. "I know exactly who you are, but I couldn't help myself once I saw you. No wonder my big brother is going crazy. You are one hot-looking babe."

She laughingly tried to bat away his arm, which seemed to have become glued to her shoulder. "I'm no babe. And yes, I am also a friend of Quentin's."

"What's that perfume you're wearing? I've never smelled anything so good in all my life."

She angled her head up at him to see if he was pulling her leg. From his rapturous expression, he seemed truly enchanted with her appearance. "Uh, I have no idea. My sisters dressed me. One of them spritzed me on my way out the door."

"Who is it, John? Are you and Harrison boxing in the foyer again?" a female voice called from another room.

"Nope. It isn't Harrison, Jeanie. It's a knock-out redhead."

Emma cringed inwardly. Oh dear. Had her sisters made her look like a fashion model? She'd wanted to surprise Quentin, but from the way his brother reacted, the surprise was on her. She reached for the doorknob. "I can't do this. I'm a fraud, John. Please give my regrets to Lucy. I need to go home."

He planted a beefy hand on her shoulder, turning her around. "Now, now. There's no reason to bolt. My family will skin me alive for scaring you off. Come on in."

With that, he maneuvered her deliberately into the family room. She reached deep for courage. Why had she ever thought a surprise would be a good idea? She didn't like surprises. Quentin wouldn't like this one either.

A wall of faces surrounded her. Quentin's stepmother, Dottie, wore a red scarf. Jeanie had a sparkling engagement ring. Alf looked like a young James Dean with his black attire. Tabby was the bubbly blonde.

Where was Quentin?

Her heart pounded in her throat. She searched the room for exits.

"Come sit by me," Lucy said, patting the sofa next to her.

"No, wait." John slung an arm over her shoulder. "Do you like baseball?"

"I've heard of the sport." Her statement loosened a torrent of information on the subject of baseball. She squirmed under the weight of his arm. Her brain struggled with RBIs and at-bats.

Quentin strolled in, and all conversations ceased. His gaze connected with Emma's. His forward momentum halted.

Expectation vibrated through the air. Her skin tingled. The silence lengthened. She'd surprised him all right.

She'd rendered him mute.

That thought brought her a small measure of joy. Mister know-it-all didn't know everything. She smiled brightly. "Hello, Quentin."

He glided across the room, knocking John's arm off her shoulder in one swift move. "What are you doing here?"

His entire family burst into laughter. She frowned at his relatives. "Lucy invited me. Would you rather I leave?"

He caught her hand. "You're not leaving here dressed like that. Who did this to you?"

She tried to take a step back, but there was nowhere to go. "Good grief. You're embarrassing me. Now your whole family thinks something's wrong with the real me."

He scowled. "Anyone who is rude to Emma will answer to me."

John leaned lazily against the wall. "I've never seen you like this, big brother."

"You were right." Lucy gave her a hug. "Quentin is snarly around you. No wonder he kept you to himself. I can't wait to watch you make him behave."

Lucy had lost her mind. Emma couldn't make Quentin do anything. She couldn't even make the lump in her throat go away. "I made a mistake. I shouldn't have come here."

CHAPTER NINE

"Don't go," Quentin said.

His deep voice rumbled through Emma, quieted her impulse to flee. She'd caused this embarrassing situation. She couldn't abandon him to his family's laughter.

Harrison, Jeanie's fiancée, arrived, and in the ensuing confusion, Quentin ushered her into the dining room. She sighed. It would be less of a fuss to stay, and she didn't want to call more attention to her or Quentin.

He sat down beside her at the table. Fierce heat radiated from him. So much for her surprise. Catching him off-guard made him mad. Worse, he seemed uncomfortable as he stole glances at her.

She'd never meant to hurt him.

All she'd wanted was to gain his attention.

She'd done that, in spades.

Turning her attention to the feast before her, she vowed to be inconspicuous. She wouldn't give his family another reason to laugh at him. She ate quietly, enjoying the sautéed vegetables and fresh bread.

"Murph called yesterday," Tabby announced. "She has a new project in mind."

Whistles and catcalls filled the room. All eyes turned to Quentin.

Her eyes narrowed. Who was this Murph, and what did she have to do with Quentin?

He shrugged. "It isn't my fault the woman has good taste in builders."

"She specifically requested you for the estimating job." Tabby grinned. "This time it's a screened-in porch."

"Ms. Murphy can request all she wants. She doesn't run Stone Construction. I'm too busy to take a look at her place." Quentin turned to John. "Why don't you send Alf out for the estimate?"

"Yeah, Alf," Lucy teased. "You keep saying you're ready for more responsibility. How would you handle an oversexed fifty-five-year-old?"

"Big brother has drummed it into our heads for years that our conduct on the job reflects on the company." Alf waggled his eyebrows. "I'd politely refuse her advances during working hours."

A hearty rumble of masculine laughter filled the room. Dottie flushed bright red. "Alf, you behave yourself."

"This particular job may require a modification of your preference for all black clothing," Lucy observed as she poured coffee. "Would you dress like Quentin?"

Alf paled. "No."

Quentin tensed. "What's wrong with how I dress?"

"You dress like Dad with your boring button-down collars and conservative neckties. Women today prefer men in styles that are relevant."

Quentin's palm smacked the table. "I don't have any

trouble getting dates. Only one woman has ever turned me down for a date."

Dottie cocked her head in interest. "And that would be?"

Emma's hand shot up of its own accord. Heat steamed from her cheeks as her arm descended. "That would be me."

"Oh?" Dottie's eyebrow arched.

Her lungs screamed for air, but she couldn't breathe. Expectation seethed around her. So much for staying out of the limelight. His family expected an explanation.

How could she tell these nice people about her father's abandonment? About her distrust of males? She'd let down her guard for Joel, and he'd betrayed her. Not exactly light dinner conversation. She gazed stupidly at her clenched hands.

Quentin's arm circled her shoulders. She nestled into the safe harbor he provided. "We decided to avoid the confusion of dating. We're friends. We're devoting our energies to her rehab," he said.

John chuckled knowingly. "You get all the breaks, big brother."

Emma looked up in time to see the frown that crossed Quentin's handsome features. "I also get the headaches, the bills, and insatiable customers like Ms. Murphy," he said.

Across the table, Dottie tsked. "How is that poor woman ever going to get her money out of that house?"

"She's not exactly poor, Mom." Tabby's blonde locks shimmered around her shoulders. "She paid in cash for her gourmet kitchen, her garden bath, her hot tub deck, and for her completely finished basement."

Harrison caught Jeanie's eye. "We need to buy her

house, sweetheart. I've always wanted my own hot tub."

"Dream on." Jeanie poked Harrison in the side. "It'll be years before we can afford a house like that. We're starting at the bottom, remember?"

Quentin nodded at his youngest brother. "Wear a tie, Alf. The woman's a sucker for a man in a tie."

Alf's eyes gleamed. "I won't let you down."

"Speaking of let-downs, where's our dessert?" John licked his lips. "I've been looking forward to this all week. Did you bring that apple stuff I like?"

Tabby leaned towards Emma. "You may not know this, but Quentin found a place in town that makes the best desserts. Every week he brings us a special treat from the shop. He won't tell us a thing about the restaurant. Wait until you taste dessert. You'll think you've died and gone to heaven."

Emma nodded politely. She had consumed entire meals from Quentin's secret restaurant, but she'd never once sampled their desserts. Odd.

"I'm looking forward to it," she replied.

Dottie and Lucy returned to the table with a stack of small plates. Dottie looked pointedly at Quentin. "Will you do the honors, Son?"

With Quentin in the kitchen, Emma's unease mounted. What she wouldn't give for a magic garment to make her invisible. Every time she opened her mouth she made Quentin the object of family ridicule. No wonder he hadn't invited her to join them.

"How did you decide to open a bed and breakfast, Emma?" Dottie asked.

Where was that invisibility cloak when she needed it? She fiddled with her cloth napkin. "I've traveled in my job at Orbital. My previous boss insisted on staying at

B&Bs, and I fell in love with the concept of an inn that was more like a home. Things at Orbital aren't great for me now, so I decided to follow my dream of opening my own B&B."

"Oh dear." Dottie's gaze wavered from Emma to Lucy. "Are things bad at Orbital for you too, Lucy?"

"Things at Orbital have been dicey ever since Joel Frazier became CEO last year. It won't get any better until he's gone," Lucy said.

Dottie fingered the red scarf at her neck. "Is your job in jeopardy?"

Lucy shrugged. "Who knows? Everyone's job seems less secure now."

"You can always come back to work for the company," John pointed out.

"Thanks. What sort of openings would Stone Construction have for a research scientist?"

"How about performing stress checks on new building materials?" Alf suggested.

Lucy nodded. "Not bad."

Quentin carried in an elegant cake topped by a single candle. Luscious red cherries dotted the top of the snowy white cake. Everyone sang, and John blew out the candle.

While Dottie presided over the cake cutting, Emma leaned over to John. "It really is your birthday?" At his nod, she winced. Lucy should have warned her. "Happy Birthday. If I'd have known, I would have brought you a present."

John cracked a smile. "How about a kiss for luck?"

Quentin dropped into his chair, frowning his disapproval.

The point of her coming here was to show Quentin she could think for herself. Impulsively, Emma leaned over to plant a kiss on John's cheek. John turned his head at the last minute, and her lips grazed his. She blushed at the unexpected intimacy.

"What kind of cake is this?" Harrison asked.

She exhaled shakily and focused on the beautiful cake. John was very straightforward about his desires. Much too straightforward for her. She scooted her chair closer to Quentin.

"Black Forest Cherry Cake," Quentin gritted through his teeth.

John dug right into the first serving. He closed his eyes in apparent bliss. "Delish. I love it."

Harrison stole a forkful from John's plate. His happy moan filled the room. "Jeanie, sweetheart, if you cook like this, I'll be your slave for life."

Jeanie licked the icing off her fingers and passed a plate to Emma. "No ordinary person cooks like this. Only Quentin's secret chef. The guy must be a millionaire. Why, I'd pay my entire weekly earnings for one of his desserts."

She took a small bite. She wasn't wild about cherry flavored anything, but she immediately understood John's blissful state. This cake tasted sinfully decadent.

"Like it?" Quentin's lips grazed her ear.

Goosebumps broke out on her arms. She shivered expectantly. Just when she thought she was used to the man touching her, her body became hypersensitive again. "Mmm," was all she could say.

John gazed mournfully at the empty serving platter. "Can it be my birthday again next week?"

Everyone laughed at his pitiful expression.

"Don't forget your presents," Jeanie said as she and Tabby brought in wrapped packages.

John tore into the larger packages with child-like delight. The shirts and ties from the females were set aside in favor of the electronic gadget from Alf, the Orioles baseball memorabilia from Harrison, and the high tech wristwatch from Quentin.

"It's getting late." Quentin stretched and stood. "We have an hour's drive ahead of us."

"Yes, we should get going." Emma rose. "Thank you for having me." Family members crowded around to hug her.

"It's been a pleasure having you join us. Come again," Dottie gushed when it was her turn.

"Why don't you come out to the house one evening? I'd love to show you around," Emma offered.

Dottie's smile filled her face. "I'll do that."

"See you in the morning, kiddo," Lucy stated.

John stepped forward to hug her. She could hardly refuse him after she'd hugged everyone else.

"You're the best birthday present I ever got," John teased, lifting her off her feet with his hug. "Except for that cake. My birthday cake rocked."

He released her and chucked Quentin on the shoulder. "Can't wait for our next dessert selection. Are you sure you won't reveal your secret chef?"

"Not a chance." Quentin tugged Emma to his side, distancing her from his brother.

Was he concerned about John? She wasn't attracted to his brother. She had her hands full with Quentin. He was the only Stone who didn't give her a hug and the one she most wanted to hug her.

"You let me know if my brother does anything to ruin the reputation of Stone Construction. This is the first time that he's taken such a personal interest in a rehab,"

Alf teased as he said goodbye to Emma.

Jeanie and Harrison intercepted them. "You're coming to our wedding, aren't you, Emma?" Jeannie asked.

"Thank you for inviting me," she ventured neutrally.

Quentin's arm curved around her shoulders. His sexy fragrance filled her head. "I'll make sure she comes," he said.

As she drove home alone, Emma realized she'd sought refuge in Quentin's quiet strength during the meal. Would he expect the same degree of closeness at the Heartly Inn? Had she inadvertently encouraged him to think she wanted to jump in his bed?

She wanted a hug.

And a kiss.

She couldn't look any further ahead than a kiss.

Dining with his family had been pleasant. They'd welcomed the cleaned-up version of Emma, but if they knew her secrets, would they be so welcoming?

She came from lousy stock. Her mother refused to fight her cancer, and her father abandoned them. Both, in their own way, gave up on life. Would she? Her grandmother had believed in her. Grandma's unshakable faith made Emma strong in her teens. It served her well during her early career at Orbital.

Now that Grandma had passed away, Emma questioned her moral fortitude. She'd never confided these worries to anyone, not even her sisters. She'd love to confide in Quentin. With her next breath, she changed her mind. He would think she wanted him to fix her problems. That would never do. No point in giving him power over her past, too.

His headlights in her rearview mirror brought her

comfort. The warm glow of good food and great fellowship resonated deep in her bones, reminding her she'd been allowed a rare glimpse of family togetherness. She could get used to feeling so mellow. Even the mounds of work to be done at the house didn't quench her good mood.

In the driveway, Zelda's kittens circled Emma's ankles. She leaned down to greet them.

She straightened, and Quentin stood before her, his muscular arms barred across his chest. "You want to tell me what that was all about?"

Her breezy confidence faltered. Danger edged the strong energy emanating from him. She chose to misinterpret his question. "I figure if my pets take the time to greet me, it's the least I can do to say hello to each one of them."

"I'm not talking about the cats. What were you doing with my family?"

Quentin was loaded for bear, and she was in his cross hairs. She shivered. "Lucy invited me to dinner. She's my friend. I can't help it if you're from the same family."

He shook his head. "You're doing it wrong. I wasn't ready for you to meet my family. I wanted things to be more settled before you met them."

He resented her initiative. So much for her taking charge of their romance. Clearly, he hated being surprised. Maybe he hated that she'd intruded into his realm.

That thought staggered her. She retreated into the safe friends-only zone they'd been in before dinner. "Settled? We're not dating. We're friends. That's what you told your family tonight," she parroted. "You're always nagging me about friends doing stuff together. I ate dinner with your family. A friendly gesture. So what?"

He stared at her. "There are certain expectations when a guy brings a girl home for dinner."

A yellow kitten looked like it wanted to climb Emma's pantyhose. Grateful for the distraction, she picked it up to keep her nylons from being shredded. "You didn't take me home for dinner. I took myself."

"I don't like surprises. I like things done a certain way. I'm too old to change my ways."

Why was he so grumpy? Dinner with his family had been lovely. From his dark mood, it appeared he didn't agree. Why couldn't he make his mind up about her?

She was in uncharted terroritory without a compass.

Heartlys weren't romantics. Moonlit kisses were a fairy tale. She should accept her lonely fate and quit dreaming about kissing Quentin.

She thrust the mewing kitten on top of his crossed arms. "I didn't ask you to change anything. It was only dinner."

He scrambled to catch the kitten, and she started up the porch steps. A thought occurred to her, a way they could each save face.

She turned back to face him. "I forgot to tell you my good news. Maddy signed the Quit Claim Deed. With a clear title, I can get a loan now. I plan to hire Stone Construction for the rehab. You won't have to spend every evening helping me any longer." She forced a smile. "Isn't that wonderful?"

* * *

Quentin blinked in surprise. His thoughts reeled from

the abrupt shift in topics. Thanks to Emma, he'd been off balance the entire afternoon. It looked like the surprises were still coming. To cover his confusion, he repeated her last word. "Wonderful."

His gut hollowed. Her ability to hire his company would put an end to his moonlighting here. In effect, he'd been handed his walking papers. She didn't need him hanging around now that she could sign a contract with Stone Construction. He couldn't openly court her in front of his crew.

This was terrible news. Why had she sprung her news on him now, when he was dealing with the repercussions of her being at Sunday dinner?

She didn't understand his position. He liked her. A lot. His family liked her. At this point in past relationships, he would have proposed, but she wasn't like his exes. She was special. He didn't want to mess this up.

He'd wanted to kiss her senseless when he saw her standing in the doorway with John. He snorted. That wasn't quite true. He'd wanted to smash his brother's face for touching her. Then he wanted to spend the rest of his life making love to Emma.

The kitten mewed in his arms. He petted it in the thickening twilight. What a mess. Emma thought of him as a friend. He wanted to be her lover.

His construction courtship had been too subtle. She had no idea of his intimate intentions, or of his deep-seated need to protect her.

He wanted to make love to her.

She wanted to be friends.

He was right back at square one.

Was he wearing down her defenses, or was she

driving him crazy? He had no yardstick to gauge their relationship. How could she ignore the strong physical attraction that flashed between them? How could she deny they were more than friends?

An oath slipped from his lips as he returned the kitten to its littermates. Nothing bothered him more than loose ends. How could he plan for their future if Emma wouldn't cooperate?

He knew what he wanted.

Emma.

In his bed.

He burned with wanting her, but she wasn't ready to commit to a diamond ring or a picket fence. He could lose her if he acted rashly. His four failed engagements reinforced the message that haste screwed things up. He had to do this right.

Life without Emma would be an unbearably lonely and cold existence. A harsh howling wind would blow through his desolate heart.

He would lose her if he didn't do something. Time to step up the pace a bit, to make his interest more apparent. He could do obvious.

But could he do it and without frightening her away?

The golf course. She'd said she would go hit golf balls with him. Not as romantic as a bower of fragrant rose petals, but this plan had one clear advantage over any other he thought up.

She'd already said yes to this date.

* * *

Emma slumped against the back of her bedroom door. It had been a near thing. He'd wanted to have a serious talk with her about their future. She'd lost her nerve. She wanted more with him, but she had to take baby steps. Right now, a kiss was her limit.

She depended on him for many things. How would she survive when he walked out of her life? Heartlys were unlucky in love. It was only a matter of time before he left.

She trusted Quentin with her life. His actions showed he was a man of his word. A real rock of Gibraltar. Unlike her father or Joel.

The real question wasn't about trusting him with her life. The real question ate at her from the inside out, gnawing at the things she held dear in her world, cutting its sharp teeth on her dream of financial independence.

She trusted him with her life.

Did she trust him with her heart?

CHAPTER TEN

Beverly lifted the whistling teakettle off the stove and poured out two cups of tea. She carried them over to the table in the bay window of the dining room. "I can't believe how different this place looks already. At the rate things are going, you'll be open for business soon."

Emma nodded in satisfaction. "Stone Construction is good, but they can't take credit for this room. Quentin and I did this. Isn't it amazing? I've learned so much about construction. If the Heartly Inn isn't successful, maybe I can buy old property and fix it up for resale. It feels darn good knowing I did this with my own hands."

Beverly put her teacup down. "Speaking of Mr. Wonderful, where is he? I got the impression he was underfoot out here like Agnes."

Emma couldn't help smiling. Quentin was nothing like her geriatric dog. "He had a family matter come up. You wouldn't believe how much they rely on each other. Someone's always having a crisis, and everyone rushes off to the rescue."

"Sounds like a television show. Does everything get wrapped up in an hour?"

"No, Quentin has been over at his brother's place for hours building a gazebo for his sister's wedding. I'm not sure when he'll be back."

"Hmm," Beverly mused into her tea. "It seems that Quentin has gone above and beyond the realm of friendship by helping out here. Now that you've hired his company, why is he still living here?"

Emma stared at her hands. "He's worried about my safety, and he's my friend. He helps his friends. His whole family is like that. Ever since last Sunday, his family has been helping us out here. His step mom is sewing curtains for the living room."

"She's sewing curtains for you while the family is putting a wedding together?" Beverly shook her head. "I don't think you're telling me everything."

She waved a hand in the air. "There's nothing else to tell. Quentin's family finds it funny when he loses his temper around me."

"Why would he do that?"

Her spirits revved with thoughts of Quentin. "He's always bossing me around. I figured out to let him have his say. Then I do what I want. It makes him a little wacky. Honestly, I don't try to provoke him, but I won't blindly follow orders either."

Her sister stirred a spoonful of sugar in her tea. "That I understand. Grandma gave up trying to tell you what to do before you hit puberty. You've bossed me and Maddy around for years."

She frowned. "I did that for your own good. If we hadn't stuck together after Grandma died, social workers would have split us up in a heartbeat. Our family may be small, but we pulled together."

"Yeah, yeah. Ancient history. Does Quentin tell you he's bossing you around for your own good?"

"All the time." She frowned and traced her finger around the rim of her teacup. "It's not that I don't listen to him about safety stuff, I do. He has these very definite ideas of how everything should be done."

Beverly chuckled. "And they're not your ideas?"

"Exactly."

"I sure wish he was here. I would love to see the two of you together. Are you certain you're not falling for him?"

That very question hovered at the edges of her thoughts. Her mask of bravado crumpled. She couldn't lie to her sister. "I don't know."

Beverly leaned forward. "I was afraid of this. Are you sure you're not overly grateful for his help?"

She slowly shook her head. "Grateful never felt like this. Grateful is a happy feeling. I'm afraid."

"How so?"

"I'm afraid that I care for him. A lot. But Heartlys don't live happily ever after. I proved that with Joel. What if I fall for Quentin, and he abandons me like Dad left Mom? I couldn't handle that."

Beverly rushed around the table and placed her hand on Emma's shoulder. "Being a Heartly had no bearing on your relationship with Joel. That guy is a jerk. Dad was a jerk, too. What decent man walks out on his family? Quentin sounds like an honorable man, a compassionate man even. I wouldn't worry about what-ifs with him. Heck, I wouldn't worry at all. Love is wonderful. Don't be afraid of it."

Fear knotted her stomach. "Love's such a big risk.

I'm more nervous about falling in love than I am about changing careers."

Her sister gave her another squeeze. "Here's the thing, Em. We don't chose who we fall in love with. It just happens. Be glad the guy you love isn't a scumbag. There are plenty of those out there."

Beverly was right. Quentin was a nice guy. She should forget her fears and accept the vulnerability that came from caring for someone. Easier said than done. She sighed deeply and cast about for a new subject. What about Beverly's love life? "Does this mean your relationship with Harold took a turn for the worse?"

Beverly rolled her eyes. "Harold roared off on his Harley to find himself. I could've told him the journey was pointless. He's looking in the wrong places."

"I thought he had potential."

Beverly walked back to her chair and slumped into it. "That's the thing. They all have potential. The trick is finding one who realizes his potential."

Emma blinked. "That's insightful. When did you get so smart?"

Her sister raised her teacup in a mock salute. "It runs in my family. I have one sister who is a genius with management. Another who is a genius with design. I had to be smart about something. I've spent a lot of your money learning to figure people out. I should be good at it by now."

With a raised palm, she forestalled any more talk in that direction. "Don't waste my hard-earned money trying to analyze me. I'm different, but I like who I am."

"That, big sister, is more than half the battle." Beverly smiled. "Most people never figure that out. You have a great future ahead of you. I'm counseling you to take a chance on Quentin."

She digested her sister's advice allow with the facts as she saw them. She wasn't trapped by her past. She'd taken steps to change her life. She hadn't abandoned her principles or her family to do it.

She waved goodbye to her sister. Beverly was right about something else. She hadn't chosen to fall in love with Quentin. It had happened of its own accord.

She loved Quentin.

Acknowledging her feelings made her lightheaded. She felt carefree. Her sister believed she wasn't cursed with Heartly bad luck with men. In fact, her sister and personal counselor had advised her to trust Quentin with her heart.

But, she'd take this being-in-love thing slowly. Quentin didn't need to know she loved him. If he didn't reciprocate her feelings, she would know soon enough.

She loved him.

The world shimmered with possibilities.

* * *

Quentin's grasp tightened on a two-by-six ceiling rafter he supported over his head. "I still think it was a bad idea to make this gazebo at your place, then haul the thing to Mom's for the wedding."

"Yeah, but Mom wanted to surprise Jeanie," John said. "The gazebo wouldn't be a surprise if Jeanie saw us building it, would it?"

"Harrison is one lucky man. He's getting the girl of his dreams next week."

John raised an eyebrow. "Still no luck with your wooing?"

Emma hadn't melted in his arms, yet. But he had plans for tomorrow. "I'm working up to a golf date. The only thing she likes so far is when I bring dinner. Then her eyes light up. She looks at me like I'm the most wonderful man in the world."

His brother laughed easily. "Hey. Whatever works. When you mess this up, be forewarned. I'm going to ask her out. Emma has something that tugs at my heart."

His temper flared. "Back off. I'm not messing this up. I saw Emma first. She's going to be mine."

John reached for the next ceiling rafter. "If you mess this up, Mom will kill you. She's practically adopted Emma."

He grumbled under his breath. His entire family believed she was the woman for him. He wanted to believe it, too. He needed to believe it. She could save him from a life of loneliness.

John grinned at him over his shoulder. "Hey, you'll never guess who called me the other day. Janice Green."

His back teeth clenched together. He'd had several calls from Janice Green himself. Calls he hadn't returned. "What did she want?"

John cleared his throat. "She wanted to know how you were doing."

Janice Green was one of the four biggest mistakes he'd made. He had no interest in ever talking to her again. Thinking about her made him shudder.

"What should I tell her?" John asked.

He shrugged. "I don't care what you tell her."

His brother stared at him point blank. "No chance you'd reconcile with Janice, and I'd get Emma?"

Quentin glared at his brother. "Not a snowball's chance in hell."

* * *

He smelled the smoke all the way out in the yard. The mantle of tiredness he'd been feeling from working on the gazebo evaporated in a heartbeat. Quentin raced up the stairs, his heart in his throat. "Emma?"

"I'm in the kitchen," she said.

Where else would she be if there was a fire? He charged into the unlocked house. The clear air confused him. "What happened? I smell smoke."

She had her back to him. Her incredible, alluring back. "Right as usual."

He noted a new pan in the yard. She steadfastly refused to discard a single burnt pan until she mastered cooking. At this rate, there wouldn't be any pots or pans left in the house. "Emma?"

She glanced at him. "Go ahead. Yell at me. I see it in your eyes. I tried cooking something other than breakfast muffins. I made a casserole for dinner, but I got distracted talking to my sister and forgot the time."

He smelled peanut butter. "I offered to bring dinner from town. Why didn't you take me up on my offer?"

She shoved a platter of sandwiches in his hand and plucked two cans of iced tea from the fridge. "I wanted to make dinner. Don't you see? I'm in deep trouble here. I'll be completely remodeled in a few weeks, but I'll only have half of what I need to run my bed and breakfast."

He wouldn't survive her learning to cook. And she might succeed in burning this lovely place down. "Hire a cook for Heartly Inn."

"I'm going to do this myself if it kills me. How's the gazebo coming along?"

Sandwich platter in hand, he led the way to her favorite spot to eat, the front porch steps. He could eat every one of her hearty sandwiches. He'd developed an overwhelming appetite for peanut butter. Maybe he'd create a peanut butter pie for Sunday dessert.

Coming home to Emma felt natural. He wanted a lifetime of dinners with her. "John and I finished the gazebo. Lucy and Tabby will paint it, then John, Alf, and I will haul it over to Mom's the day before the wedding."

"Jeanie is so lucky to have you guys helping with the wedding."

"You make it sound like I had a choice." Quentin munched through another sandwich. He grimaced at the metallic taste of the canned iced tea. He should've made a pitcher of tea before he left this morning.

"Of course you had a choice. You could have been out hitting golf balls or something else that was fun. Instead, you spent your evening building a surprise for your sister. That's sweet."

Her praise irritated him. "Sweet? Think again. I do what has to be done to keep peace in the family."

She shook her head solemnly. "You can't fool me. I've known you for over a month now. You're a sweet man. You help people out. And you don't have any ulterior motive. That's so sweet."

His thoughts about Emma weren't sweet. They bordered on erotic. "I'm not sweet. I'm a man, and right now I smell like one. I need a shower."

She laughed and waved her sandwich at him. "Silly. I wasn't talking about body odors, but I like the way you smell. You have an honest scent about you, like you've been working hard all day in the fresh air and sunshine."

He narrowed his gaze. Something was definitely up.

She'd bestowed two compliments in five minutes. Personal remarks were topics she avoided. Body odor qualified as personal. He felt his way through the conversational maze. "I like the way you smell, too."

Her face scrunched up. "I don't smell like anything special. I don't even own a bottle of perfume."

Did Emma want to deepen their relationship? Had she finally given him a green light? Hope made him bold. He tugged her to her feet. "You don't need perfume, Red. Your natural scent drives me wild."

She blinked rapidly.

He offered her his hand. "How about a walk out to the lake?"

She cautiously joined hands. "We didn't finish the sandwiches yet."

Her fingers seemed so delicate, but he knew of their strength. "I'll secure the food in my Jeep. Nothing should bother it in there."

Emma smiled up at him, and his heart flooded with longing. "Good idea."

Crickets chirped beside the grassy path. Moonlight shimmered invitingly across the surface of the quicksilver water. The urge to kiss her welled up inside him. He halted in front of her. "Kiss me."

Her hand jerked in his. "Now?"

Dang. Had he misread her signals?

Go for it, he thought. He nodded. Agonizing seconds ticked off his life.

"Isn't that a little premeditated? Like asking someone if it's all right to kill them? Why can't you be spontaneous about a kiss? Why not do your typical man of action thing and kiss me anyway?"

He massaged her hand with his thumb. "You mean

too much to me. I don't want to rush you. You've kept your distance for a long time now, but tonight you aren't afraid."

Her feminine chuckle sounded mysterious. "I've never been afraid of you, Quentin. I've always known I could trust you. The problem is me."

He blinked. "What?" She stepped closer to him, but he waited impatiently for her response.

"I haven't had great luck with men. Early on, I was too busy raising my sisters to date. The man I dated in college was only interested in the fringe benefits of our relationship. I tried a romantic relationship recently, but it blew up in my face. I'm cautious with good reason. The women of my family have historically chosen the wrong men. It's like we're cursed."

Her arms circled his waist. She clung to him. He held her close. He wanted to do something violent to the men who'd hurt her. "I can't speak for the other men in your life, Emma. I don't run from problems, but my dating luck hasn't been much better than yours. I've been engaged four times. I have four ex-fiancées."

She laughed so hard she choked. Alarmed, he pounded on her back.

"Four engagements?" she asked. "Do you ask every woman you meet to marry you?"

His arms dropped to his side. So much for true confessions. She would never melt in his arms at this rate. "I thought I had feelings for them, but those feelings can't compare to what I feel for you. I want so much with you that I'm afraid to even begin telling you about it for fear of ruining everything."

Her hand stroked the side of his face. He leaned into her palm, wishing and hoping she cared for him.

"You're afraid of me, too," she ventured. "I wondered if that might be the case. I've discouraged masculine attention over the years so that I could achieve my career goals. I hid behind too-big clothes and a can't-be-bothered attitude. Neither of those things put you off?"

"Wear whatever you like. It won't change how I feel. All I ask is that you take a chance on me."

"You have to take the first chance."

He took a deep breath. "Will you go golfing with me? Will you kiss me?"

Her arms lassoed his neck. Her lips touched his, hesitantly at first. He kissed her back, drawing her sigh of acceptance deep inside himself. She tasted of peanut butter and woman, and he hungered for both. Her curves nestled into him.

Like a dieter treated to the vision of a luscious dessert, he craved her delights. He wanted to touch her all over, to find bliss in his arms, to hear his name upon her lips.

He gave himself to the pleasurable sensation of exploring her mouth. Her wildflower fragrance infused his lungs as his fingers threaded through her curly hair. With his fingertips, he traced the sleek planes of her cheekbones, reveling in the smooth slide of her skin under his fingertips.

She was sweetness and light.

She sparkled in his arms.

Emboldened, he drew her closer, kissed her deeper. He'd been right about the passion in this woman. It surged out of her like two-twenty current. The powerful charge zoomed through him, tripping his internal circuit breakers right and left.

He loved it.

He wanted more.

Later, he promised himself.

One step at a time.

He ended the kiss. "Nice," he whispered.

"I'd like to do that again," she whispered back.

"Given both our track records, we'd better take this slow and easy."

She laughed. "Are you putting our relationship on one of your famous schedules?"

It was his turn to laugh. Happiness surged through his veins. "I've waited weeks to hear you say that word. It feels great to have you admit we have a relationship."

"I'm used to doing things at my own pace. I don't like being told what to do or when to do it."

"You're not going to make this easy for me, are you?"

"No. But I won't make it difficult either. I'll be myself. That way you can't blame me if this doesn't work out."

Catching her hand in his, he headed back to her place. "Oh, it's going to work out all right. Because you won't try to change me into something I'm not."

"Spare me the lecture. I'm not an ex-fiancée."

He felt lighter than he had in days, years even. "Pack a suitcase tonight. We're moving into my place in town while the work crew sands and refinishes the floors. And I'm taking you to the driving range after work tomorrow."

She stopped walking. "I can't leave here. I have animals that need feeding."

She didn't want to go with him? His gut twisted. "John will camp out here while we're in town. Agnes,

Zelda, and the kittens will be fine."

"He'll feed them, but will he talk to them? Will he fuss at Zelda for catting around? Will he praise Agnes for being a good dog? I don't think so. Besides, it's a bad idea to stay with you if we're going to be more than friends."

He wanted her sleeping under his roof. "Those sawed joists are serious. Until we catch the person who sabotaged your floor, I want you to have someone you trust with you all the time. I don't want your sisters or mine drawn into this. If someone is after you, they're going to have to go through me to get to you."

"Gosh, that's so romantic. What did I ever do before such a big strong man came into my life?" She batted her sexy eyelashes at him and huffed out a lungful of air. "Forget it. I'm staying here."

He swore under his breath. Why couldn't she accept what he said at face value? "This is for your own good. Breathing in the fumes from the floor finish is unpleasant. Stone Construction recommends our clients vacate their homes when we refinish wood floors."

"Why didn't you say so? Why did you try to order me around?"

He sighed. "I honestly don't know."

She patted his arm in consolation. "There's hope for you yet, Quentin Stone."

CHAPTER ELEVEN

Emma called Maddy from the privacy of her bedroom. Desperation threaded through her voice. "What do people wear when they go golfing?"

"Hi, Emma," Maddy said with suspicious good cheer. "Isn't Beverly your wardrobe shrink?"

"I figured I'd cut out the middle man this time. Go straight to the source. If any of us had been to a golf course, it would be you."

"Right you are. I've never played golf, but I attended a business luncheon at Bulle Rock over at Havre de Grace a few months ago. The chef there is divine."

Emma dragged her suitcase out of the closet. Every place had a great chef these days. Every place except the Heartly Inn. "What should I wear?"

"Back up a minute. Since when did you take up golf?"

"You know good and well I didn't take up golf. Quentin talked me into going to a driving range with him."

Maddy's silence irritated Emma. "You still there?"

"Yeah. I'm here."

"What's wrong?"

"What's wrong is that you've got a date, and I am between men."

Was her sister jealous? With Maddy's social whirl, Emma couldn't imagine her sister sitting home alone at nights. "I thought you were seeing someone."

"He was a client. He dropped me once the job was done."

"Sorry to hear that, Maddy."

"I should have picked up the loser vibes much sooner." She sighed. "That's neither here nor there. Let's get you rigged out for a golf date. You've got some sneakers that aren't full of paint?"

"I've been painting in my bare feet. My sneakers are good to go."

"Good. All you need is a shirt with a collar and a pair of khakis."

"A collared shirt?" She thumbed through the hangars in her closet. "Like my white blouse?"

"Try a polo shirt instead."

Relief washed through her. "I have a couple of those. Thanks for the advice."

"About Quentin—"

She held her breath. "Yes?"

"He seems like a decent guy."

"You approve of him?"

"If he's what you want, go for it. I don't know how you stayed away from men so long anyway. Nothing wrong with a good romp in the sack."

"I tried the romping part years ago, and it wasn't satisfying." She sank down on her bed and hugged a pillow to her tummy. "I want more from a relationship than the physical union. I want someone who will stick with me when bad things happen. I don't want to end up with a man like Dad who cuts out at the first sign of trouble."

"Every woman wants that. Trying to find that level of commitment in a sexual partner is difficult. Everything is disposable these days, relationships included. That's why the singles scene is so popular at nightclubs."

"I refuse to be someone's lay of the week. Forget that. If I can't find the right guy, I'll stay celibate the rest of my life."

"Quentin will take care of that if you give him a chance. He looks like a man that knows his way around a bedroom."

She blushed. They'd strayed too far into her private life for her taste. "Speaking of Quentin, he's moving me into his place tomorrow night. They're sanding the floors here. He says I need to stay out of the house for a few days."

"Stay here with me instead."

"Those saw marks on the floor have him spooked. He doesn't want you, Bev, or his sisters drawn into danger. I can't bear for anyone else to be hurt. It felt awful knowing I'd put Lucy in harm's way before."

"Gotta say this about your guy. When he makes up his mind, it's full steam ahead."

"No kidding."

"Kind of convenient for him to have this excuse to keep you close. You okay with that?"

Her love for him glowed brightly in her heart. "Yeah. I'm okay with that."

* * *

Quentin lowered her suitcase to the carpeted floor of his bedroom. How often had he pictured this moment? It seemed he'd been angling to have Emma in his bed ever since he met her. "You'll stay in here. I hope you don't mind that I only have the one bathroom. We'll share it."

She stalled in the doorway. "I shouldn't put you out like this. I can stay on your couch."

Her hesitation irritated him. He took a deep breath. This wasn't about sleeping with her. This was about protecting her. He focused on that goal. "Out of the question."

"Why is it out of the question?"

"First, I have to be at work earlier than you do. If you slept on the sofa, I'd wake you up. Second, I'm not letting this nut get to you. I'll be staying between you and the door."

"This is so weird." She shivered. "I can't believe anyone is after me. Or that they would find me here."

When he kissed the top of her head, the coiled red curls tickled his nose. She didn't sink against him the way she had out at the lake. In fact, her arms didn't encircle his waist at all.

Bringing her here had spooked her. He'd have to let her get used to the idea of being here, of sleeping in his bed, of living under his roof before he asked her for more.

Because he surely wanted more, much more.

His hands trailed down her elegant spine, wishing the time was right. His gut instinct told him to have patience. He hadn't listened to his instincts with his previous fiancées. This time would be different. This time he was paying attention.

With regret, he stepped away from her. "While you're in the bathroom, I'll move a few personal items into my weight room next door. Feel free to hang up your clothes in the closet."

The thought of their clothes sharing closet space seemed very right. Soon they'd share more than a roof. Soon they'd share his bed.

* * *

"We'll start out on the practice green." Quentin motioned toward the level grassy surface adjacent to the parking lot.

Emma veered off towards the tee boxes on the hill. "You said there was nothing like watching balls soar off the tees. Isn't that where we have to go?"

"We'll get to that. Putting is easier."

She stopped moving altogether. "You don't think I can hit the ball?"

"No. That's not what I said at all." He slung his golf bag off his shoulder. The legs of his collapsible bag stand folded out to support the bag. "I want this to be fun for you. And I need to practice my putting."

He needed the easy start, not her. She relaxed enough to smile. "Why didn't you say so?"

Putter in hand, he strode briskly over to an unoccupied corner of the green. He demonstrated a short putt for her. "The idea of putting is to roll the ball in the cup."

His ball sank in the hole. She could do this. "It's like putt-putt."

"Shhh. Golfers take this sport seriously," he warned

in a husky whisper. "How far the ball travels depends on the slope of the ground, the speed of the playing surface, and the amount of force applied to the ball."

He dropped another ball onto the grass. He walked around the green, holding the putter like a plumb bob.

Under cover of her lashes, she studied the other golfers' attire. Maddy had been right about the polo shirts and the khakis, but the nonconforming footwear gave her away. Hers were the only sneakers among the two-toned oxfords. Her heart sunk. Did the other golfers know she'd never done this before?

She needed to think of something else besides her inadequacies. Her thoughts turned to the question that had been bothering her for days. "Why did you ask *four* different women to marry you?" she blurted out.

His arm jerked. The ball veered left of the hole. His gaze darkened. "Rule number one of golf etiquette is no talking when a person is in the process of striking the ball. Your turn."

Chagrined, she accepted the club he offered. "Does it matter how I hold it?"

"Find a grip that feels natural. Make sure your eyes are over the ball before you hit."

"Like this?" She took a large-radius practice swing. The other two golfers on the green headed for the tee. She was alone with Quentin in the practice area.

"Keep your arms straight so the club head hangs from your shoulder like a pendulum."

She swung the club with rigid arms. "Is this better?"

He rolled a ball over to her. "Not bad. Show me your stance again. Address the ball, but don't hit it."

"Huh?"

"Addressing the ball is your position prior to hitting

the ball. Let me show you." He snugged up behind her, placing his hands over hers on the putter. He guided the putter in a couple of practice swings before tapping the ball into the hole. "See. It's easy. You try it."

Her heart thudded in her chest at the sensory overdose. Kinetic energy hummed from their contact points. She drew in breaths of him hungrily, savoring his brisk woodsy aroma.

Her golf ball rocketed into the hedge. She wanted to die. "This is the easy part?"

He tapped three balls over to her. "Try it from close in, gradually increasing the distance to your target. Putting is about feel."

She herded the balls with her putter. "I thought you said putting was about distance vectors and the force applied to the ball."

"That, too." He stroked two balls into a nearby hole before he gave her his full attention.

Conscious of his gaze, she applied herself to the task of a two-foot putt. One of her three balls sank in the hole. She chewed her lip. Putting was hard.

"That's good," he said. "You're getting the hang of this."

Her accuracy improved, but the mental challenge didn't hold her attention. It couldn't when Quentin was nearby. This was their first date. They should be getting to know each other better.

"Why four fiancées? Did you get a group discount?" she asked, forgetting the no-speaking rule.

His putt scooted right. "God help you if you put those four in the same group."

Her voice softened at his ragged tone. Those women must have hurt him bad. No wonder he wanted to take things slow with her. "Did you fall in love with all four of them?"

"I thought so, but I was wrong."

Conversation settled her nerves. She rifled another ball into the cup. "But *four* women? What happened? Why didn't you marry any of them?"

"It didn't work out."

"Why not?"

"They wanted to change me. And there was one other minor thing."

Ah. The truth at last. She arched an eyebrow at him. "What's that?"

He exhaled slowly. "They thought I was bossy."

She laughed until she couldn't see straight. Wiping the tears from her eyes, she faced him squarely. "Forgive me. I wasn't laughing at you. Those women didn't know you very well. Why were you so keen on marriage?"

"The timing seemed right," he began. "I had my own place, the business was doing well. My family didn't need me around so much. Once John took over some management aspects of the firm, I realized there was more to life than work, but something was missing in my life."

"You thought it was a wife? I would've thought you could have any woman you wanted."

"Getting them wasn't my problem," he qualified. "I couldn't keep them. Once I spent time with my exes, I realized we had little in common."

She cocked her head at his wry tone. "So, you asked them to return your engagement rings?"

"They threw the rings at me." He grinned. "They couldn't get away fast enough."

"I don't understand." She frowned. "You're a great

friend. You're fun to be around. You're good in a tight situation. How did you go wrong four different times?"

His grin faded. "Beats me, but I wouldn't date any of those women again. And, I learned my lesson about engagements. Never again."

She digested his words. He didn't want anything to do with his exes. He was soured on engagements. He was focused on the present. On her.

She smiled inside.

After sinking an eight-foot putt, she raised her arms in a victory salute. "I've mastered putting. What's next?"

"What about you?" He studied her. "I can't believe a man hasn't asked you to marry him yet."

"Believe what you will. I haven't had a single proposal. I've been too busy to have a social calendar. Working fulltime during college cut into my social life. I dated a physics major for a year, but he dropped me for a doctoral candidate who had more free time. Afterwards, I was busy with my sisters, getting them through school and helping them launch their careers. I've worked for Orbital for ten years, and my responsibilities keep increasing and eating up my evenings. I thought that would change when I dated Joel, but he was the biggest mistake of my life. Looking back, I'm not sure why I dated him."

"Do you still love him? Even though he made you feel like chopped liver?"

Her putter slid through her fingers. "I never loved him."

"It seems to me you're holding a torch for this guy, especially since you haven't dated anyone since him."

"Joel is a first-class jerk. End of story."

He shrugged. "You can't blame me for asking. Why

stop dating altogether? Did someone else also treat you bad?"

He deserved to hear all of it. She wanted to tell him. Would he hold her family secrets dear?

She longed to be open with Quentin. She was in love with the man. She should tell him. Sighing, she reached for the club she'd dropped. "Yes, there was someone else. My father."

"Your Dad?"

His sharp tone ignited her temper. "We don't all come from perfect families like yours. Some of us hail from dysfunctional families. We carry that burden everywhere we go."

He moved heart poundingly close. "Did your father take advantage of you in some way?"

She retreated off the green at his outrageous question. Revealing family secrets was harder than sinking that white ball in the narrow holes. She cleared her throat. "Not in a physical way. Nothing like that. But parents leave other wounds."

"Don't keep me in suspense. What happened?"

The intensity in his gaze held her entranced. She'd never told anyone about that horrible time. Not even Lucy knew about her family's secret shame. "It's embarrassing."

He arched an eyebrow. "More embarrassing than having four ex-fiancées?"

She broke free of his gaze to stare at the lush carpet of grass. Cars whizzed past on the highway. Birds sang in trees. It was an uneventful evening for everyone else.

She took a deep breath. "Daddy walked out. One day he went to work. He never came home. He didn't want us anymore. It was terrible."

"Where did he go? Did you ever see him again?"

Her throat clogged. She hated what her father had done to the family. "I don't know where he went. He left twenty years ago. Vanished. He made no effort to contact us. You can see where I might have a history of distrusting males."

His face tightened into an angry mask, concerning her. Did he think less of her now? Why had she thought this was a good idea? What madness had caused her to bare her deepest secrets? She may as well have been standing naked in a crowded city park.

"Not every man would walk out on his wife and family."

"On his dying wife and three young kids." Her stomach twisted into a tight knot. "My mother officially died of breast cancer, but she quit fighting it the day my father left. My eighty-year-old grandparents lived on a fixed income and were in declining health. Overnight, I had to figure out how to take care of all of us."

He whistled under his breath. "I can see where you might have trust issues."

"My sister Beverly studied psychology to better understand why he left." She stubbed the toe of her sneakers in the short grass. "I've often wondered how much of my father I have in me. I wonder if I'll one day walk away from someone I care about."

He pulled her into his arms. "You're not your Dad. You're not a quitter. You're the type that goes down with the ship, sweetheart."

She took comfort in his embrace. With her ear pressed to his chest, she heard the steady beat of his heart. "How do you know that?"

"How many quitters would single-handedly

undertake the renovation of that old farmhouse you call home? How many quitters put their sisters through school? I've seen you in action. You work hard. You don't shy away from trouble."

Heat rose to her cheeks. He believed in her. He wasn't ashamed to be seen with her. Even if their romance fizzled, he'd be her friend. The warmth of his caring circulated through her body. "Thanks. It's great having a friend like you."

His arms tightened before he released her. "Let's get a bucket of range balls," he said.

She handed him her putter. "Cool."

An hour later, she still tried to hit the junked cars on the driving range. Quentin joined in the game with his sand wedge and hit the nearest car on his first attempt.

"How'd you do that?" she asked.

"Practice."

"You sure it isn't the club? I think you've been holding out on me, keeping that W club all to yourself."

He flashed a toe-curling smile and handed her the club. "Give my wedge a whirl."

Aware of his gaze resting on her, she tried to remember the things he'd taught her. Arms like this. Hands like that. Turn at the waist. She swung fast and missed completely. "Oops." Heat flooded up her neck. "Guess you were right. It wasn't the club."

"You rushed the shot. Swing easy, and you'll have it."

She glanced down at the mat. One ball remained. She glanced at the car again. "Will you help me? I really want to hit that blue car."

"Sure. Go ahead and address the ball."

She held her breath as he wrapped around her, his

hands clasping hers on the club. Her goal of hitting the car receded. She'd much rather forget about golf and focus on her golfer.

"We'll take it back nice and slow." He guided the stroke. The ball launched off the tee. Seconds later it plunked on the roof of the blue car.

Joy surged through her. She turned around and high-fived him. "Yeah! You did it."

"We did it."

"That felt great."

He slid his wedge back into the golf bag. "We'll have to do this again."

"I'd like that. I had fun today."

"Me, too." They walked to his Jeep. "Did you hear from the police today?"

She faltered in mid-stride. He steadied her. He seemed to be doing a lot of that lately. "Yes. They've interviewed my sisters and my coworkers at Orbital. They have no leads on who sawed my floor in two."

"You can't think of anyone else who might be upset with you?"

She shook her head. "I can't think of anyone. I avoid further conflict by keeping my head down. I stay too busy to get into much trouble."

"I want you to always carry your cell phone. If you're going to be late coming home, call me so I won't worry."

"Worry wart." She playfully punched him in the shoulder. "I'm not used to being held accountable for every action I make. You're making too much of the potential danger."

He lowered his golf bag from his shoulder and unlocked his Jeep. "I'm being cautious until we know what this is all about."

"Sounds like you're being bossy to me," she grumbled.

"That's me." He grinned. "Bossy. It's what I do best."

She groaned. "It wasn't a compliment. I'm complaining. You should at least get mad at me for fussing at you."

"It's a balmy summer evening. I've spent an hour at the driving range with a beautiful woman." He opened her car door. "What's there to be grumpy about?"

She sighed. "What indeed?"

She should be happy someone cared enough to be worried, but his constant hovering chaffed. He meant well, she knew he did. But he didn't need to fret over her. He had a business and a family to worry over. She'd been looking out for herself for a very long time. She wasn't about to stop now because he wanted to worry about her.

She had other things besides safety on her mind. Like their fledgling romance. Was one kiss enough for him? Why didn't he try to kiss her again? Had she inadvertently put distance between them? How did she ask that question without sounding forward?

He acted different now that they had moved into his condo. Less relaxed, more uptight. Did he have regrets? In his protective mode, he was always alert. Instead of soothing her, his constant watchfulness sent frissons of awareness through her.

She had standards. She wouldn't make a bigger fool out of herself by throwing herself at him again. She'd content herself with holding his hand for now.

She was not a desperate, love-starved thirty-year-old. Just because she hadn't had sex in eight years didn't mean she had to jump the first interesting guy to come along. She'd vowed to take that step again only if it had deeper meaning.

Romance shouldn't be one-sided. By kissing him, she'd indicated her interest. Quentin needed to make the next move.

CHAPTER TWELVE

A little after five the next afternoon, Quentin strode down the empty corridor of Orbital Scientific, intent on finding Emma. Last night in his condo, he'd decided against kissing her goodnight, afraid that things might go too far. All day he'd been thinking about the missed opportunity. He was here to amend his mistake.

His heels echoed down the drab institutional corridor. Darkness filled the first two doorways he passed. Lights blazed from the sampling lab, bringing a smile. He'd suspected Emma would be hard at work.

He knocked on the door as he opened it. "Emma?"

She turned from her paperwork, her lips edging up at the corners. A white coat swallowed most of her, with only her trim ankles and strappy shoes visible. His heart sped up at the sight of her, and her smile brightened the lonely places in his soul. His instinct to come here had been right on the mark.

He slowed a bit, savoring her scent and the way her eyes rounded with welcome. Warmth flowed through him. He longed to hold her in his arms.

Instead, he brushed his lips against hers. She opened her mouth for him, dizzying him with the prospect of more. One hand slid behind her neck as he drew her close.

From the soft feminine sound she made, she'd been thinking about kissing him, too. He slanted his lips over hers, tasting and testing as she yielded to him. His blood swam with need.

With reluctance, he broke off the kiss. "I thought we could grab some dinner."

Emma rose. Her hand brushed against her throat. "Dinner? I hadn't thought that far ahead."

She seemed stunned, bemused even. He'd never had that effect on a woman before. "It comes around every day right about this time."

"What are you doing here?"

He gave her hand a reassuring squeeze. "I was in the neighborhood, so I thought I'd take you to the Red Dragon."

A petite woman with multi-colored hair emerged from the rows of hissing machines. "Emma, aren't you going to introduce me to your friend?"

Emma's entire face turned bright red. "Sure. Heidi Moore, meet Quentin Stone. He's been helping me with my rehab." She turned to Quentin. "Heidi works with me in the Sampling Lab."

He nodded to the woman, aware of her taking his measure. She looked like the kind of girl his younger brother Alf would bring home. Pierced eyebrows and ears. Probably a tattoo on her plus-sized cleavage.

"I might be in the market for some rehab soon," Heidi stated. "Do you have a card?"

He released Emma's hand to retrieve his card. She used the opportunity to skitter away from him. "Give Stone Construction a call when you're ready for an estimate," he told Heidi.

"Roger that. Night, Emma." Heidi strolled out the door, fanning herself with his card.

Behind him, Emma checked the drawers of her desk. One drawer closed with a loud bang. He shot her a worried glance. "You okay?"

"No, I'm not okay. You're at my job. This is my other life. I don't mix my work life and my private life."

He noted that she didn't say social life. His heart sunk a little. "I'm getting mixed signals from you. Are you ashamed of me?"

She huffed out a breath of air. "No. Why would I think that?"

How could a brilliant woman miss the facts that were right under her nose? "I don't have a college education. I work with my hands."

"So what? College isn't for everyone." She grabbed his elbow, hustled him out the door, locking the lab behind her. "Don't try to manipulate me into feeling sorry for your lack of formal education. You run your own business, for heaven's sake."

He walked her out to the parking lot. In the few minutes he'd been inside, the lot had emptied. "People are serious about quitting time here."

"You would be too if you worked for Joel." She fumbled in her bag for her keys.

He nodded towards his vehicle. "Let's take my Jeep. We'll pick your car up on the way home."

She nodded, and he breathed a small sigh of relief. She'd said she wasn't embarrassed to be seen with him, but other than their golf date they hadn't been together in public. On the plus side, she hadn't protested today's kiss.

Tonight, he'd kiss her again, making sure he had her full attention.

* * *

Emma rushed across the condo threshold. "That's such a shame about your favorite restaurant being closed. Your family will be disappointed come dessert time on Sunday." She was talking too fast, but she couldn't seem to help herself.

Her confidence had tanked during dinner.

"Mmm." Quentin locked the door behind them.

She wrung her hands. During dinner, she'd sensed a storm gathering. She was not prepared for a storm. Especially if the storm was named Quentin.

The tension in the air thickened. She moistened her lips. Her clothes were mixed with his in the closet. Their toothbrushes shared a cup in the bathroom. Did he intend to share her bed tonight?

Her flight instinct took hold. She dashed into the living room, skirting the coffee table as she circled the room. He caught her on her second lap.

"Are you running from me?"

"Yes. I am." She shot him a worried glance. "You make me nervous."

"You make me hot."

His deep voice rumbled through her, further inflaming her nerves. "When you say things like that I get confused. Anxious, too."

"It's okay. I'm feeling a lot of emotion myself.

Physical attraction flows between us like an electric current. Can you feel it?"

She shivered. "Yes." Wanton thoughts crowded her mind, making her wish she wasn't cautious. She wanted to draw him near, wanted to melt against him.

Rallying, she squared her shoulders. "I'm not into casual sex."

"Sex between us would not be casual. It would be extra-ordinary." His voice softened in entreaty. "Come to me, Emma. Spend the night in my arms. You won't regret it."

Her head twitched in denial. "No casual sex. I'm firm on that."

"Are you a virgin? Is that why you're on edge?"

The consideration in his voice irritated her. "I've been in a slump since college. Trust issues, remember?"

"Ah, I see. That explains a lot, sweetheart."

"Don't." She thrust her palm in his direction. "Don't seduce me with endearments, or anything else in your dating arsenal. I'm on the verge of changing careers. I can't risk dividing my concentration."

"It doesn't have to be an either-or situation. You can have both."

"So you say, but you've never walked in my shoes. I can't afford to fail. If I do, I'll jeopardize everything I've ever wanted."

He kissed the underside of her wrist. "I promise you can call the shots. I'm going out of my head with wanting you. I want to kiss you good night."

She shivered again. "I-I-I can't think."

He moved in, clutching her palm to his chest. "No thinking required. Kiss me. Please."

The scents of pine trees and man filled her head.

Beneath her palm, his heart beat steady. His heat enveloped her. God help her, she wanted to kiss him more than anything.

She brushed her mouth against his, reveling in the heady excitement of touching him.

"Again," he urged in a ragged voice. "Kiss me again."

His magnetic pull proved irresistible. She kissed him, her arms slipping around his waist. His arms encircled her. He tasted exotic like the apple pie they'd shared, cinnamon spicy and caramel sweet.

Her hands stroked down the corded strength of his back. Along the muscled biceps of his arms. She nestled closer, thrilling to his hard planes.

Instinct urged her to close the final gap between them. His hands feathered up her spine. She arched into his caress. His thumbs traced the lower edge of her bra.

It wasn't enough.

"Emma," he whispered hoarsely against her throat. "Are you sure?"

With a start, she realized her hands were on the third button of his shirt. She jumped backward, miraculously missing the coffee table. With that kiss, she'd gone from a clear-headed career woman to a woman enthralled by desire.

Mere seconds ago, she would have sacrificed her future for the exquisite feel of his bare skin against hers. Her responsibilities and goals had melted in the flash fire of passion. Dear heaven.

Quentin followed her retreat, matching her step for step. "Because if it isn't what you want, we're about to reach the point of no return."

The heat in his eyes called to her, but her brain

rebooted. They were about to cross a line she'd drawn in the sand, one she'd vowed to respect until she was sure of a man's commitment to her and their future.

"I need to stop." She glanced down at the taut fabric of his trousers. She'd never had this effect on a man before. "What about you?"

"What about me?"

"Are you, uh, uncomfortable?"

"I'll survive." Satisfaction gleamed in his eyes, giving her pause. "But not if you keep looking at me like I'm your second dessert."

"Oh!" She dropped her gaze to the floor. Her wants were at a crossroads with her needs. She wanted to make love to him, but she needed more from him than sweet words and recreational sex. She needed to know he'd stick through thick and thin.

"In that case, I'll see you tomorrow." She managed a decent exit to his bedroom with no hysterics or running, though that's what she felt like doing, even after she closed the door.

His touch had driven all thought from her head. Desire had chorused through her blood as it never had before. She could practically taste it. Was Quentin the man she'd waited for? Would he stay with her when times were tough?

She wanted him.

He wanted her.

A basic, instinctive reaction to unleashed passion.

She could go back out there and finish what they'd started. It would be so easy. It would be so freeing and fun.

But she wouldn't know if he was the one.

He'd taken on the task of protecting her. Didn't that

mean he cared?

Joel had said he cared, but look where that had gotten her. Nowhere. Quentin wasn't Joel, but who would he be in the long run?

A keeper?

Or a loser she should've tossed back?

* * *

"These samples came from a construction site, Miss Green?" Emma had been overwhelmed when the buxom blonde barged into the sampling laboratory. Miss Green's stylish attire looked out of place in the plain setting.

Miss Green's perfectly aligned teeth were visible under her bow-shaped lips. "Yes. There was standing water on two of the lots we're developing. The water had an odd color to it. The odor was foul. That's why I brought these samples in." A set of salmon pink nails waved over the top of the two mason jars of crystal clear water on Emma's own little bit of counter.

Her fingernails were flawless. How irritating. Equally annoying was the exact color match between her pink nails, clothing, and accessories.

Something else about this woman bothered Emma. Was it the way Miss Green looked down her nose at her? Was it the intense scrutiny Emma felt from her?

A bug under a microscope wouldn't feel more exposed. Which made no sense at all. Why should the very beautiful Miss Green care about Emma's appearance?

Regardless, she had a job to do. She assigned sample numbers to the jars and pulled out some forms.

"Did you check with the county to verify the history

of the lots in question?" Emma remembered an instance in the news several years ago where a company had been found guilty of midnight dumping. The company had sought to avoid the expense of paying for hazardous waste disposal by spraying their waste material on abandoned property under cover of darkness. The composition of the waste had led investigators back to the industry, and the executives were charged. Orbital analyzed those samples, although that was before Emma's assignment to the sample department. Old timers at Orbital still talked about helping the police solve the case.

Thoughts of playing environmental detective danced in her head. Maybe there were hidden benefits to the sampling department after all. She collected the remaining required information. Miss Green signed the manifest. Emma couldn't wait to tell Lucy about these samples. They would get the kid glove treatment.

Miss Green shoved a business card at Emma. It boasted the same nauseating shade of pink trimmed with a green logo and green lettering. "Please call me as soon as possible with the sample results. These work crews have been temporarily reassigned to other Green Construction job sites."

Emma read the fine print under the mountain range logo on the card. Miss Green was no ordinary sample courier. She owned Green Construction.

"Our analysis time runs about three weeks. Unless you want to pay extra for rush service."

"Three weeks? That won't do. We have performance stipulations in those contracts. We can't be three weeks behind schedule." Miss Green ramped up the wattage on her cheesy smile. "I'll need that faster service you mentioned."

Emma pulled out a rush authorization form. "If you'll sign here, we'll begin processing these samples immediately."

Not a hair on the blonde stirred as she leaned down to sign her name. What must it be like to go through life perfectly groomed? How much time did it take each morning to achieve perfection?

Not that she would take the time to fluff herself up each day. Too many other important things to do. Emma waved her lab assistant, Heidi Moore, over from the gas chromatograph. "These are rush samples. Process them immediately. Full EPA priority pollutant panel."

Heidi gave Miss Green a second and a third look. Emma made a mental note to ask Heidi's opinion of their new client later. Her assistant often had very interesting insights into people. "Sure thing, boss."

Emma gave the perfect Miss Green her brightest smile. "Okay. You're all set. You'll have a verbal response in forty-eight hours, an audited report in a week."

The perfect Miss Green didn't move.

Trying to ignore her, Emma straightened the stack of completed reports on her desk. She'd hoped to finish reviewing these reports this morning so they could go out in the afternoon mail. "Was there something else you needed, Miss Green?"

Miss Green's salmon nails fluttered at her throat. "This is a bit awkward. I hoped we might speak privately."

What could the two of them possibly talk about? Did Miss Green have a future need for a bed and breakfast? "There's the break room down the hall. We can talk there."

"Great."

Emma led the way to the empty break room. She closed the door behind them. "What can I do for you, Miss Green?"

"First, I insist that you call me Janice. I feel like we have so much in common."

"Oh?"

She almost laughed aloud at the woman's absurd statement. Instead, she stuck her bluntly cut fingernails in the deep pockets of her comfy lab coat. She blew an errant strand of curly hair out of her field of vision. From her transparent vinyl pocket protector to her no nonsense black pumps, Emma had little in common with Miss Janice Green.

Miss Green delicately cleared her throat. "It's come to my attention that you're acquainted with Quentin Stone."

Emma's heart sunk. She wanted to discuss Quentin? "I'm not big on cryptic remarks. I'm a linear thinker. Please speak plainly."

"I see he hasn't put a ring on your finger yet. When I heard he was dating you, I felt compelled to tell you the truth about Quentin."

Emma narrowed her gaze. "Who are you?"

A stricken look crossed Janice's face. "I'm crushed that you don't know me. I'm fiancée number three."

Her throat tightened. Quentin had been engaged to this gorgeous creature? On her best day, she couldn't hold a candle to this woman's beauty. She struggled to regulate her rapid breathing. If she kept hyperventilating, she would surely pass out.

"And?"

"And, I'm trying to save you the awful embarrassment of being engaged to Quentin Stone. The man is a nasty user. You need to know that before you go any further with him." Janice sighed. "I wish someone had done me the same favor a year ago."

Emma didn't want to hear Janice's version of dating Quentin. "Your fears are unjustified. Quentin and I are friends. Marriage isn't part of our discussions."

"That's not like him at all. With all of his previous fiancées, he put a diamond ring on our fingers within a week of meeting us. Once he had the wedding scheduled, he changed from an incurable romantic into the most impossible tyrant you could imagine."

"Maybe he learned from his mistakes."

Janice's salmon-colored fingertips fluttered through the air. "I don't understand. You're living in his condo."

Emma retreated behind a mask of civility. "Are you so desperate for a man that you spy on him?"

"I don't spy on anyone. Construction is a small world, and I hear things. That's all."

She wasn't buying the woman's story. "Quentin is my friend. I don't appreciate your unprofessional comments about his personal life. Please keep your comments to yourself in the future."

"If you change your mind, let me know. There's plenty I could tell you about Quentin Stone."

"I need to get back to work." Emma nodded toward the door, and the woman departed.

A shudder traveled down her spine. She'd held her own against Quentin's former fiancée, but it hadn't been easy. Dealing with the woman had left a bitter taste in her mouth. At the tap on her shoulder, she startled.

"I wondered where you went," Lucy said. "Was that

Janice Green walking down the hall?"

Emma nodded, trusting Lucy with her observation. "Her name should be Janice Pink."

"What did she want?"

"She brought in water samples, which now that I think about it, are probably tap water, but she paid twice the going rate to have them rush-analyzed."

"Good for us. Joel will be happy about that." Lucy pinned her with a sharp look. "And?"

"She wanted to warn me about your brother."

"Oh dear."

"Oh dear is right. She views Quentin as a love-'em-and-leave-'em type of guy. She warned me against becoming engaged to him."

Lucy growled deep in her throat. "Quentin won't like this."

Emma huffed out a breath. Did no one appreciate that she could talk care of herself? Quentin wasn't her keeper. "Don't tell him she came by. I can handle an ex-fiancée."

"He'll be upset that Janice sought you out. Heck, I don't like it either. Janice is preoccupied with two things: Janice and Green Construction. She wanted to marry Quentin so that he could take over her paperwork, and she could run the company."

"He must have hated that."

"Yeah. When he wouldn't go along with her plans to merge the two construction companies, Janice went a little crazy. She made a big scene in a downtown restaurant when she dumped my brother. I still have nightmares about having Janice for a sister-in-law. Thank goodness that engagement ended."

"He can do a lot better than a selfish person like

Janice. He deserves someone nice and nurturing. I could tell that wasn't her style. Plus, she came across as dictatorial. That would clash with Quentin's bossiness."

Lucy nodded. "Janice wants a man she can keep on a short leash, one who doesn't question her right to wear the pants in the family."

"Sounds like you know her pretty well."

"Our fathers worked together years ago," said Lucy, "so we knew Janice as a child. She brought over her entire universe of Barbies when we played together. Between Tabby, Jeanie, and I, we had two Barbies. We weren't allowed to touch any of Janice's dozen fashion dolls. Later, when Janice came home from boarding school, she wowed all the men with her curvy figure, but under all those layers of pink, she's still self-centered Janice Green. She always rubbed me the wrong way." Lucy took two sodas out of the refrigerator, offering one to Emma. "At first I thought it was because I hate pink so much. But then I realized my dislike went much deeper than that. I want to muss up her perfect hair, or, at the very least, splatter phenolphthalein on her shiny outfit. How's that for a mature reaction?"

"Perfectly understandable." The cola soothed Emma's parched throat. Better yet, it nullified the foul taste of her previous visitor. "She seemed very keen on telling me about Quentin. If I hadn't been firm and suggested she leave, I imagine she'd be here telling me all kinds of things about your brother."

"My brother is easy to figure out," Lucy said. "On the other hand, Janice has always been a piece of work. I have a sneaking suspicion she ruined it for Quentin and Amy."

"Amy?"

"His fourth fiancée," Lucy explained. "He met her at a trade show, got engaged a week later, and got unengaged two days after that. She gave him his ring back. Told him she never wanted to see him again. I'll bet you anything Janice talked with Amy."

"Sounds like Amy might've had second thoughts about such a hasty decision. I've got to ask. Lucy, what is it with these whirlwind engagements? From what I've seen, Quentin isn't in a rush about anything."

Lucy grinned. "He's changed since he's met you, Emma. My family thinks it's a good thing he's taking the time to be friends with you. We believe he has strong feelings for you."

Emma chewed on her lip. He wanted to sleep with her, but that wasn't the same as love. "You think I'm going to be number five on his engagement list? Don't think that for a minute."

"I can't help it. I want Quentin to be happy. He's done so much for the rest of us. Now it's time for him to be happy."

"We're friends."

"Yeah. Right." Lucy made a show of glancing at her watch. "Let's order pizza in for lunch today. I'm on a tight schedule."

"Okay by me. Hawaiian pizza?"

"Deal."

Emma returned to the sampling lab. Heidi had printed the bar-coded labels for Janice Green's samples. They attached the labels to the sample vials. "What do you think about our new client, Heidi-Mo?"

Her lab assistant twirled her safety glasses. "You're referring to the ethereal vision swimming in pink curves? The woman Walt will be dreaming of for the rest of his natural life?"

With a quick glance over at the love-struck technician loading the automated sampler for the mass spectrometer, Emma nodded. "Yes. That woman. I want the unadulterated Heidi-Mo report."

"She's not your long-lost friend from childhood, is she?"

"I've never set eyes on her before today."

Heidi exhaled loudly. "Just checking. I wouldn't want to lose my job over something I said. I'm into political correctness in the workplace."

"Quit stalling. I already told you that you're the best there is. What did you really think of her?"

"She's a piranha in heels. Steer clear of her, boss lady. Her kind goes for the throat every time."

Something loosened in Emma's chest. "We're in complete agreement. Enough said." With confirmation from Lucy and Heidi, she knew her first instinct had been correct. Janice Green was trouble. Poor Quentin. He'd been engaged to a piranha. "You up for Hawaiian pizza?"

"I'm up for a free lunch anytime you're buying. Count me in." Heidi grinned. "Nothing better than pineapple and ham on pizza."

Emma called in the delivery order and plowed her way through the sampling reports. It wasn't easy to concentrate. Her thoughts kept returning to Janice Green. If Janice was Quentin's type, what did he see in Emma?

She wasn't glamorous.

She didn't run a construction business.

She was plain old Emma.

How could she hold his interest after the house rehab? She'd known from the start that he loved the farmhouse. Maybe that's all they shared, a mutual interest in fixing up the Heartly Inn. That and a strong physical attraction.

One thing was for certain. Emma couldn't be Janice Green. Oh, she cleaned up nice, but beauty pageant glamor wasn't her style. She was more the roll-up-your-sleeves-and-get-to-work type. Hard to know what Janice looked like when all the war paint came off.

Janice flashed and sparkled.

If Quentin went for glam, Emma's future looked bleak.

CHAPTER THIRTEEN

Knowing Quentin slumbered in the next room kept Emma awake for hours. She couldn't stop thinking about him. She had visions of slipping into something sheer and clingy, the likes of which she didn't even own.

Thoughts of inviting him to join her in his king-sized bed wouldn't leave her alone.

Sleep, when it finally overcame her, was fitful.

When she stumbled out of the shower the next morning, Quentin had already left for work. She was very late and feeling sleep-deprived. If she caught all the stoplights right, she might make the staff meeting on time. She dashed out to the parking lot.

She stopped short, staring in disbelief at the flat tires on her reliable Saturn. Four flat tires. How was that possible? Mindful of her business attire, she crouched beside the deflated left front tire. She fingered a slash in the black rubber. Her blood turned to ice at the sight of four additional cut marks.

She glanced around the lot, seeing trees, bushes, and

vehicles. How did this happen? Quentin lived in a nice, upscale neighborhood. Vandalism shouldn't be an issue here. Heart in her throat, she surveyed the other vehicles parked nearby.

Not one flat tire in the bunch.

Was Quentin right?

Did she have an enemy?

The warmth faded from the bright summer morning. Every shadow, every hiding place seemed full of danger. Emma ran for the safety of Quentin's condo. With trembling fingers, she dialed Quentin's number.

"Lock the door. Call the cops. Stay inside until the police come," he commanded. "I'm leaving the jobsite now."

She clung to the phone. "Okay. Thanks."

She called the cops. Then she called Lucy. "I won't make the staff meeting. My car—" Her throat squeezed shut. Panic raced through her body.

"Oh, no. Is it your battery again?"

"My tires were slashed." Emma sucked in another shallow breath, trying to calm herself. She was safe. Nothing had happened to her. Just her car. Purposefully, she drew in a deep breath. "First the sabotaged floor. Now this. Quentin was right. This is personal."

"Good Lord. Do you have any idea who did this?"

"That's the nerve-wracking part. The only person I know of that doesn't like me is Herb Goodlow from R&D. But Herb's a scientist, not a terrorist."

"Hmm," Lucy said. "I agree with you about Herb. Something is a little off there. I'll keep an eye on him."

Emma choked out a strangled laugh. "I thought you were already keeping an eye on him, so to speak."

"He's not interested in dating me, that's for sure. I've

dropped enough hints that even a blind person could've noticed my interest. So, something must be wrong with him because nothing is wrong with me. He should want to go out with me. I know he's always here when I leave at night. There's nothing that fascinating in the R&D lab that would cause anyone to work overtime without pay." Lucy sighed. "But we'll worry about Herb later. If I don't get going, I'll miss the staff meeting. Bye."

Emma hung up the phone. In Lucy's paperback romances, the leading lady often drank hot tea after an unsettling event. Good idea, she thought.

Quentin's kitchen cabinets brimmed with cookware. She rooted through gadgets she couldn't name until she found a smallish pot. After adding water, she set it on a burner to heat up.

The warmth of the stove took the edge off her inner chill. Where did he keep mugs and tea? She opened cabinets to find what she needed. The jar of peanut butter next to the alphabetized spice rack brought a fleeting smile to her lips. Quentin must have purchased the peanut butter for the nights when it was her turn to fix dinner.

Finding a third frying pan sparked her curiosity. How many frying pans did he own? She opened every cabinet and counted nine frying pans in all. Why would anyone have so many?

Her lungs stilled at the faint scraping sound at the front door. Was it her car assassin? Her fingers closed around the handle of a medium-sized cast iron skillet. She hid behind the kitchen door and held her breath.

"Emma?"

She exhaled in relief at Jeanie's familiar voice. She set the heavy pan down on the counter and hurried to Quentin's sister.

"I'm sorry about your car." Jeanie enfolded her in a hug. "Quentin sent me over to keep you company."

She wiped the tears from her face. Black mascara smudges dotted her fingers. She wished she wasn't allergic to the waterproof kind. "I'm sorry to put you to any trouble."

"Don't worry. I had to come here anyway today."

Her sympathy touched Emma. Tears welled in her eyes and she let them fall. It felt good to cry.

Was she cracking up? It wasn't like her to get so emotional.

In moments, Jeanie had them both seated on the black leather sofa. Through ugly sniffles and ragged gulps for air, Emma tried to explain. "I'm sorry. This is so unlike me."

Jeanie nodded understandingly.

Words tumbled forth seemingly of their own volition. "My life feels like it's been flipped upside down. Everywhere I turn, something isn't right. I want to quit my job, but I have bills to pay. My house is in a bigger mess now that the rehab is under way. And there's this thing with your brother—"

"What thing with my brother?"

She blushed. "We're becoming very good friends. I don't know what you think about me staying in your brother's place, but let me reassure you. Quentin is a perfect gentleman."

"He is?" Disappointment tinged Jeanie's voice.

Emma nodded. "He's an honorable man."

"It's not my place to say anything," Jeanie continued, "but that's never stopped me before. The entire family believes you're perfect for Quentin. How do you feel about him?"

"I've fallen in love with him." She sighed. "I didn't want to fall in love. I tried not to have any feelings for him, but I can't help myself."

Jeanie's smile radiated her approval. "I'm glad to hear that. Quentin's had miserable luck with women, but he's so happy with you that we believe his luck finally changed for the better."

Emma blew out a puff of air to move a clump of hair from her face. "I don't know how he's been with anyone else. I only know how he's been with me. Thing is, I don't understand why I love him. He bosses me around, and he's taken over my life. Worse, I've let him."

Jeanie gazed wistfully at the glittering diamond on her finger. "I know exactly what you're saying. Harrison tries to boss me around. The man had the nerve to suggest I give up all my male clients from my cleaning business. Can you believe it?"

Her eyes widened. "Gosh. Did you do it?"

"Nope. You've got to take a stand on the things that are important to you."

"I can't complain too much about the things Quentin tells me to do. Most of them are things I planned to do anyway."

"Love is a funny thing." Jeanie twisted her ring aound her finger. "I've known Harrison my entire life. At first, he was John's friend and hated me tagging along with them. Then one day he asked me to a school dance. After that, he came over to see me instead of John. We dated the entire time Harrison attended college."

"And you're getting married next weekend."

"Yes. The trick is staying out of Harrison's way so we don't have a fight before the ceremony. I love him, but the man can make me cross-eyed with anger."

Emma nodded.

A crisp knock sounded on the door. Emma blinked at the abrupt noise. The morning's events came flooding back into her thoughts, along with another wave of fear. With Jeanie behind her, she opened the door for the cops.

"Tell us what happened," said the taller of the officers.

Emma recited her discovery of the slashed tires. She couldn't stop shivering. "Does this sort of thing happen often in this neighborhood?"

"No ma'am," the cop said. "It would help us out if you knew of someone who had a grudge against you."

"I don't have any enemies. I'm a scientist, for Pete's sake. Nobody gets mad at research scientists."

There was the scrape of a key in the lock. "Emma?" Quentin asked, hurrying into the condo.

"We're in the living room," she answered.

"You all right?" His gaze ate her up as he approached. He marched up to her, his arms enfolding her shoulders.

Relief spiraled through her, warming her, healing her. "I am now."

His arms tightened around her for a moment. He introduced himself to the cops. "What's your take on this? Is this related to the vandalism at her inn?"

"Tell us about the prior incident," the heavy-set cop said.

Emma savored his touch during his accounting of the sawed joists. He'd been the one she wanted when trouble appeared, and he'd come right away. He cared for her, that much was obvious. But what if bad things kept happening to her? Would he continue to be supportive?

"Are the incidents related?" Quentin asked. "This

feels personal to me."

The tall cop nodded. "We asked Miss Heartly about enemies. She had no names to offer. It might be helpful if she mentally retraced her steps for the last few days. A name might occur to her."

She thought about it, and a name popped into her head. Funny how brains worked when they weren't fried with terror. "I had a visit at work from Janice Green yesterday. I wasn't sure what to make of it at the time, but she acted unhappy about my relationship with Quentin."

"Janice Green?" the tall policeman asked, writing down the name.

"My ex-fiancée," Quentin answered for her. "Why didn't you mention her visit last night?"

She shifted under his penetrating gaze. Was he upset over the visit or her omission? "I didn't say anything because I handled it. She didn't threaten me. All she wanted to talk about was you."

Quentin rubbed the back of his neck. "I've known Janice for years. She's all talk. I can't believe she slashed your tires."

The cops exchanged a significant look. "We'll check into it. Anyone else?"

Once again, Emma gave out the contact information of her family and coworkers. The policemen left after promising to keep them informed of any progress on the case.

The tension in the room thickened. Emma tried to make light of the situation. "What do you want to bet that the deductible on my auto insurance is the same amount as the cost of replacing the tires?"

"Do you belong to a car club?" Quentin asked

Emma.

"No. I don't take trips. Why would I need a car club?"

"Because they're good for times like this." Quentin dialed his car club and arranged for Emma's car to be towed.

Jeanie sniffed the air suspiciously. "Do you smell something?"

Emma's stomach sunk at the charred scent. The stove. She dashed for the kitchen. Quentin's empty pot was jet black on the bottom. Wordlessly, he reached around her for a hot pad, removed the pot from the stove, and turned off the red-hot burner.

"I'm sorry," Emma choked out.

He opened a window to air out the scorched smell. "What is it with you and cooking?"

Emma wished the floor would open up and swallow her whole. "I have good intentions, but cooking doesn't hold my interest. I thought a cup of tea would settle my nerves, but once everyone arrived I forgot the pot on the stove."

"Have you ever set fire to your lab?" Jeanie asked with a worried look in her eye.

Emma raised her gaze to Quentin's furrowed brow. "No. I'm embarrassed about making this mistake. I'll replace your pot, Quentin."

"It can be salvaged." His eyes sparkled dangerously. "And you can clean it. Maybe if you scrub one of your disasters clean it will help you remember next time."

"An educational experience? Why didn't I think of that?" Emma summoned a thin smile.

"About Janice," Quentin began.

Emma groaned at the name. "Everything about her

irritates me. I can't believe you were engaged to her."

"I'll talk to Janice," he said. "She won't bother you again."

Why should he take care of her problems? She solved her own problems. "I know you mean well, but I would rather you didn't. Speak to her, that is. Let the cops handle this. If Janice is behind these violent acts, they'll take care of it."

He steered her out of the kitchen. "I'll think about it. In the meantime, why don't I drive you to work so Jeanie can get started cleaning?"

Work seemed like a sanctuary compared to her out-of-control private life. "Thanks. I'll bum a ride home from someone at work."

He shot her a stern look. "Until this is over, you stick with your family or mine. Don't trust anyone else. If Lucy is busy, arrange for a ride with someone else in the families."

"Everyone else is guilty until proven innocent, eh? That's the democratic spirit," Emma climbed into his Jeep. "How did you get here so quickly?"

His lips twitched as he backed out of his parking space. "I'm thankful the police were investigating crimes and not patrolling the roads."

* * *

"Miss Heartly. Come in. Sit down." Joel gestured to a chair in his office.

Had she fallen down a rabbit hole? His voice sounded sympathetic. How amazing. Emma sank into the plush armchair.

She'd expected Joel to be angry. A Joel that acted

like a decent person took the wind right out of her sails. "Vandals slashed my tires this morning. I'll take leave for the time I missed from work today."

"Don't worry about it." Joel waved her offense away with a casual flip of his wrist. "I have something important to discuss with you."

His casual attitude put her on edge. "You do?"

"It's fortunate that you came in today. I've scheduled two more business dinners for you to attend."

Her spine stiffened. "Please ask one of the other department heads. My after-hours schedule is full these days."

Joel steepled his fingers. "Ah yes. The new boyfriend. Well, no matter. Make adjustments to your social calendar. I require your presence at dinners on Friday and Saturday of this weekend. I'll pick you up."

Emma turned cold inside. Saturday was Jeanie's wedding. Friday night was the rehearsal dinner. She'd been invited to both. After everything Quentin had done for her, she wouldn't stand him or his family up. "No."

"No?"

The shock in his tone made Emma's stomach roll. Even so, Joel needed to understand she wasn't at his personal beck and call. "I'm not available this weekend."

He sat up straight. "No?"

"No." She rose to her feet.

"Need I remind you that your future at Orbital is on the line, Miss Heartly?"

Maybe it had been a bad idea to come to work today. The emotions of the morning simmered in her bloodstream. Her temper flared. "Don't make idle threats. My job performance is exemplary, but if you think you have due cause, fire me."

"Emma, I need you. Our relationship—"

She planted her palms on his desk. She leaned toward him. "We don't have a relationship. Forget about dating me. I'm not *ever* going out with you again, for business or pleasure."

His mouth dropped open.

Why didn't she have a camera to record priceless moments like this? Emma took a mental snapshot. She labeled it "CEO rendered speechless."

She breezed out of the office in a wave of righteous indignation. She should have been much firmer with Joel in the past. Her insides churned with energy.

Heck. She was a new woman.

She had a future that didn't involve Joel Frazier, a future bright with promise and friends. Lucy was her friend, regardless of what happened with Quentin. True friendship was a rare gift she would never throw away.

Joel was a user. She didn't trust his generosity concerning her tardiness today. To cover her bases, she headed straight to the personnel office to sign for today's leave. That way he had nothing to hold over her head.

Until she had an income stream coming in from her bed and breakfast, she needed this job. No matter how she looked at it, her days at Orbital were limited. Her heart beat rapidly at the prospect.

CHAPTER FOURTEEN

"Thanks for the ride home, Luce." Emma buckled the seat belt in her friend's Volvo. "I'll have my car back tomorrow."

Lucy eased out of the Orbital parking lot onto the access road. "I thought Quentin didn't want you to be alone until this nut gets caught."

"He's heavy into bossing me around. But I learned something today. I won't cower. If I live in fear, I've lost the freedom to live my life. I won't let this nutcase take my freedom."

Horns honked in the rush hour traffic. "I agree, but I know my brother. He's keen on safety. He won't allow you to dash about unprotected."

"I'm grateful to his mechanic for fitting me in today. Without that, I wouldn't have my car fixed yet. I'm cooking dinner tonight, to even the score. After that, I'll have a clean slate. Quentin will have to like it or lump it."

"You should be home free with the applesauce and the bagged salad. You remember what we talked about for the hamburgers?"

"Yeah. Sear them for a few minutes on each side. Piece of cake."

"Honestly, you run the lab like a tight ship. You should run a kitchen like one of your sampling machines."

"Interesting that you should bring that up." Emma glanced down at her clenched hands. "Heidi thinks my cooking problems relate to my troubled childhood."

"Oh?"

"She thinks I had a cooking trauma back then, something that is deeply buried in my subconscious."

Lucy peered over the top of her sunglasses. "We've never talked about your childhood before. I know you shouldered responsibility for your family as a teen, but I never knew the circumstances. Will you tell me about it?"

She stared out the windshield at the white lines on the road. "It feels like yesterday. My sick mom. My missing dad. I called my grandparents to come get us."

As she remembered that fateful day, the smell of charred food made its way through her memory. "Dad's supper heated in the oven overnight. The next day, it was burnt to a crisp."

"That's traumatic all right. Why didn't you tell me about this before?"

"I didn't put it together before now. Plus, I'm ashamed of my dad."

"Your dad wasn't a caring father." Lucy paused to change lanes. "Heidi may be onto something. If you associate cooking with that event, I can see where you might want to block it out."

They rode a while in silence until Lucy slowed to turn into the condo parking lot. "Look at that. Quentin is already home." She shot Emma a wry glance. "There goes your surprise dinner."

She gathered up the grocery bags from between her feet. "Not necessarily. I can be persuasive when I want to be."

"My money's on you." Lucy waved goodbye. "See you in the morning."

She dashed up the stairs and unlocked the door, breathless. "Quentin?"

The mouthwatering smells emanating from the kitchen made her stomach growl. Quentin emerged from the kitchen, a huge scowl marring his face. He wore a white apron over his clothes. "What are you doing home an hour early?"

A startling revelation dawned on Emma. He didn't have a favorite restaurant. He'd been cooking all the wonderful food. She laughed so hard she couldn't stand up straight. The grocery bags slid from her hands. Tears of mirth streamed down her face.

Without a word, he closed the door. He collected the spilled groceries, a wary expression on his face. No wonder. His precious secret was exposed.

She wiped the tears away. "I came home early to surprise you. I surprised both of us."

Uncertainty clouded his eyes. "Emma?"

"The cat's out of the bag now, Quentin. I know all about your favorite restaurant. It's right here in this condo, isn't it?"

He nodded slowly. "You're right."

His hawk-like gaze didn't intimidate her. She couldn't imagine why he'd kept his cooking a secret. Did he think people wouldn't like him if he cooked like a dream? She tugged one of the grocery sacks from his hands. She tried to skirt him. He blocked her way.

Though she met his level gaze, her heart melted at his turmoil. "It makes no difference to me if you can cook or not. Why keep your talent a secret?"

"Because."

She hated seeing him in pain. She lowered her groceries to the floor and touched his arm. "I'll keep your secret, if that's what you want. I would never do anything to hurt you."

As long as they were sharing secrets, she wanted to share hers with him. If she continued to wait for him to make the next move in their relationship, she might be waiting forever. "I've never told anyone this before." She touched his chest. "I love you."

Heat flared in his eyes. He hugged her close. She melted against him. Thank goodness he wasn't disgusted by her emotional confession. She allowed herself the luxury of dreaming he returned her feelings. Tears of joy seeped through her lashes.

He kissed away her tears and claimed her mouth. A tiny doubt wormed through her happiness. Why didn't he say something? Was he telling her by his actions?

In her heart, she knew the truth.

He loved her.

Why else would he put up with her?

A familiar charred odor filled the air. Emma nibbled on his ear. "Something's burning."

With a muttered oath, Quentin ran for the kitchen. Emma followed. His kitchen looked like a high tech assembly line. She watched him move briskly about the room. "Why did you keep this a secret? How many hours does it take you to make those fabulous dishes?"

He switched on the exhaust fan. "Not long if you're

organized. The hard part is cleaning everything up before you or a family member notice anything."

"But Quentin, cooking is a *good* thing. It's something I want to learn. I can't believe you'd keep it a secret."

"Cooking is okay for a woman. There's the little matter of my construction company."

Puzzled, she sat down on a barstool. "What's gender got to do with anything?"

Quentin handed her a glass of iced tea. "Lots. Most men don't cook."

"That's not true. Many top chefs are men."

He snorted. "I'll bet you none of them own construction companies."

"So what?"

"You don't understand. Guys have limits, you know, certain things they should do. They get a lot less respect if they do things that women are supposed to do."

"So? You're the boss at Stone Construction. Fire them if they don't respect you. Have your crews ever eaten any of your cooking?"

"Well, no. I've been too busy cooking for you and making Sunday desserts and working two jobs to feed any of them."

Emma laughed. "Is that all?"

He pulled her into his arms again. "Is that all? I've been making myself crazy trying to get you to fall in love with me. I can't believe revealing my cooking secret brought you to your senses."

Before he kissed her again, his eyes narrowed. "Wait a minute. Maybe you only love me for my cooking?"

She covered his hand with hers. "I like your cooking, but I love you because of who you are. You're a wonderful man. You've made my dreams come true. How could I not fall madly in love with you?"

He paced the room. His abrupt retreat fueled Emma's abandonment anxiety. He'd wanted her to fall in love with him. She'd done that. Why was he unhappy? Was her negative Heartly karma playing out before her eyes?

Was this awful mud-sucking feeling in her gut what her mother felt when her father vanished?

"How do I know this is real?" Quentin asked from over by the sink. "Four other women claimed to love me, but they didn't mean it. Don't you want to change me?"

"I like you fine the way you are. Except for the bossy thing. But I understand that."

His eyebrow arched. "You do?"

"Sure. You've been the head of your family for a long time now. You're the one they look to for answers, you're the one who makes the big decisions. I understand because the same thing happened to me. I didn't choose to be the head of the family. As the oldest, I inherited that role. Why do you think I want to work for myself?"

"Because you hate following orders?"

"Exactly."

He rubbed the back of his neck. "Then it won't work out between us. How can two people who are used to being in charge possibly get along?"

"I don't know about you, but I'm highly motivated to make our relationship work. Shouldn't we focus on our strengths? I'm good at organizing. From the looks of this kitchen, so are you. We both put everything into our work, so we have strong work ethics. And, family is important to me. I learned to place a value on that from you."

He closed the gap between them. "You did?"

"Yes. You taught me that hovering is not a bad thing. That caring about someone means you go out of your way to help them. You've been doing that since you met me." She flashed him a bright smile that reached clear down to her toes. "I've always been a quick study."

"What do we do now?"

How would he respond if she suggested they delay dinner for a sexy romp? Could she cope with rejection if he dismissed the idea? She swallowed thickly and chose a safer topic. "We work on dinner together. You can teach me how to cook."

"What about your dinner? What were you going to cook?"

Was that regret flitting through his gaze? Had he wanted her to suggest a non-cooking activity? "Nothing fancy. Why don't we put my fixings away and work on yours tonight? We can cook my burgers tomorrow night."

"All right." He fisted his hands on his hips. "As long as you understand that I'm the boss in this kitchen."

She gave him a quick kiss. "You can be the boss of every kitchen we're in. Do you think I'll get fat if I eat your cooking all the time?"

His eyes twinkled with mischief. "John advised me to keep you fed with food from my favorite restaurant. He said that would win your heart."

"John was right. If I'd have known you could cook like this, I would have kidnapped you on sight."

Quentin fiddled with some bowls on the counter. "Why don't you wash the spinach while I chop up these boiled eggs?"

"Okay." She slid off her stool. "I discovered something else today. An event from my past came to mind. Something I haven't remembered in years. What would you say if I told you I subconsciously sabotage my cooking because of an event that happened when I was a kid?"

"Why would you think that?"

"Because there's no logical explanation for my cooking disasters. I can't remember the first thing about what I'm cooking, but I can keep endless data points in my head on any other topic."

"I'm not good at this kind of touchy-feely thing. I'm lucky to know what my emotions are most of the time."

She dumped the spinach in the lettuce spinner and gave it a whirl. "I've been going about this all wrong. Self-analysis is like a scientific experiment, only all the data has already been collected. I've never thought about sorting through my memories to figure this out."

He finished chopping the eggs and mixed the salad dressing. "What if you figure it out? If something in your memory blocks your cooking efforts, how will knowing that help you? I don't get it."

"Don't you see? If I can prove to myself I don't have anything to lose by cooking, maybe I won't have the problem any longer."

She dumped the rinsed spinach in the salad bowl. "Where did you get all of the carryout containers for your meals? I can't believe you pulled this off for so long."

He flashed a bone-melting grin. "I bought the containers at a restaurant supply place. I have them in every conceivable size."

"But why the big deception? Why wouldn't you let your family know about this?"

"My father didn't cook."

Her brain clicked into high gear. Here was something else they had in common. Past events in their family had shaped their view of cooking. Granted, their reactions to the events weren't similar, but it forged another link between them. "So, in order to be like your father, you couldn't cook. What did you say before? Most men don't cook? Ha! One man didn't cook is more like it. Your cooking shame stems from your childhood."

"Don't get carried away with this psychoanalysis thing. I had a great childhood. My family is terrific. I wouldn't trade it for anything."

"I'm not asking you to give them up. Sheesh. My point illustrated another commonality. Our lives and our decision-making processes were shaped by our childhoods."

"Give it up. Everyone faces obstacles. Only wimps spend their whole lives blaming their parents for stuff. We are what we are."

"Gosh. Who knew that a construction guy could be so deep? I'm impressed."

"I may not have a fancy college degree," he added, "but I know people."

"All right, Mr. Amateur Psychologist. Why do you think I can't cook?"

His knife sliced through the carrots. He gazed briefly at her. "I don't think it's a good idea for me to give you my opinion. You'll only get mad at me."

"Getting a little warm over there? They say if you can't stand the heat, stay out of the kitchen. Come on," Emma pressed. "It won't hurt my feelings. I'd like to hear why you think I keep messing up."

He dumped the chopped vegetables in the sauté pan. "This is a bad idea. This is how I messed up four other relationships. You don't want my opinion. You want something that I can't give you, fiction."

She edged in front of the stove. "I'm not one of those other women. I deal in black and white facts all day long. The only fiction I know about exists between the pages of the romances I read. I won't walk away if you tell me something I don't like hearing. Promise."

He exhaled loudly. "Did you ever stop to think that cooking facts can't fit in your brain because you've got too much other stuff up there? A lot of smart people can't chew gum and walk. You've got a lot going on upstairs. Plus, your survival never depended on your cooking. You get by with tangential foods like peanut butter, cereal, and cottage cheese. If your life depended on it, you could cook."

Emma absorbed his words. He thought she was smart. That was good wasn't it? Some guys were threatened by smart women. Not Quentin. He thought she could cook if she had to. Not bad for a free opinion.

Now it was her turn. "That's pretty good. Have you ever considered you went into the wrong line of work?"

He shook his head in denial. "Not a chance. Construction's in my blood. There's nothing I like better than fixing up old homes. Your house is a classic. The way it's put together is fascinating. Your great-grandfather used materials that lasted longer than his lifetime, maybe even our lifetimes. I love old places like that."

She bit her lower lip. He loved her house? Did he love her? Was this his way of telling her that he loved her? Why couldn't men express their feelings? Everything would be so much simpler if they did.

* * *

That night, Quentin stared at his living room ceiling. Emma wasn't repulsed by his cooking. She thought it was wonderful. He'd shared his opinion on personal topics, and she hadn't walked out on him.

He couldn't stop thinking about her, but did he *love* her?

What was love anyway?

Why couldn't two people like each other and that be enough? Love made a man vulnerable. It certainly wasn't a smart course of action. If a man went through the motions of love, everything hurt less.

He should know.

He was an expert at going through the motions of love.

Because he was afraid. Loving Emma was a risk. If he loved her, it would hurt too much when she left him. He'd be better off holding his heart in reserve.

Just because she thought she loved him, that wasn't a good reason to get engaged. No way. Engagements were the first step to ending a relationship. He couldn't risk that.

But he needed to be more than friends with her. Holding her hand and kissing her weren't enough for him. Her fiery passion sparkled through every movement she made, but he respected her inherent caution too much to sleep with her until he had this all worked out.

Emma *was* different.

He cared for her.

Boy, did he care.

He felt more protective of her. More possessive. More generous with his time. And she loved him.

It was a miracle.

But was it *really* love?

CHAPTER FIFTEEN

His soufflé fell.

Emma was over an hour late coming home. Quentin tried her office line again. Her voice mail clicked on. He couldn't keep his growing fear out of his message. "Emma? I'm worried about you. Please call me if you've been delayed at the office." He called her cell phone. Her recorded message came on immediately, which left him more unsettled. She always took his calls.

Where was she?

How would it look if he went to her workplace to check on her? He had due cause for concern. Someone had tried to hurt her twice now. Even though he wanted to keep her in a bubble, he realized she had to go to work each day. His fingertips tapped on the table.

He'd felt this gnawing uncertainty once before. When Emma and Lucy fell through the floor. He didn't believe in any woo-woo nonsense, but he couldn't afford to ignore it either. Not if Emma's safety was at stake. He snatched his car keys from the credenza and took off.

He made steady progress through the cross-town traffic. What if whoever sawed those beams and slashed her tires had gotten to her at work? Why hadn't he been more forceful in assuring her safety?

He knew the answer. He didn't want her to accuse him of being too bossy. But he couldn't help himself. He was bossy because her safety meant everything to him. He couldn't let anything bad happen to her.

Why hadn't he insisted she call him before she left work each day? He would suggest that very thing right after he yelled at her for worrying him.

He pulled up behind her Saturn in the mostly empty Orbital parking lot. A red Mercedes sports car parked near the building entrance was the only other vehicle. The thought of her working late with her boss set his teeth on edge. He didn't think much of Joel Frazier. He'd be glad when Emma quit this job.

He opened the unlocked door and hurried to the sampling lab. His footsteps echoed down the empty tile corridor.

The restless feeling worsened. An icy chill filled his gut. He walked faster. He had visions of horrible laboratory disasters, chemicals boiling over, toxic fumes wafting from the laboratory. Anything was possible with Emma.

Machines blinked, buzzed, and beeped in her illuminated lab.

"Emma?"

Where was she? Had she gone off with her boss? He opened drawers at her desk until he found her purse.

A wave of relief washed through him. No woman went anywhere without her purse.

Was she in Frazier's office?

Anger pulsed through him. He hated that she worked for a tyrant. While he didn't know the man, photos of Frazier in the business section of the paper had shown him to be self-assured and well dressed. Like Emma, Frazier had graduated from college. They worked in the same field and understood complex scientific principles.

He closed the drawer containing her purse and studied her desk. This workspace differed from his world. These rows of high-tech machines and thick volumes of procedures might as well be a foreign language. Hell, he couldn't even pronounce the chemical names on the blank sample form on her desk.

He'd bypassed college to step into his father's shoes at the family business. He'd rallied his siblings, and together, they'd built Stone Construction stronger than ever. He was not a lesser man for his lack of education.

The cooler air of the lab cleared his head. Why was he jealous of her boss? Emma loved him, not her jerk of a boss.

He returned to the corridor. She was here somewhere. He would find her. He passed the darkened Research and Development lab. As he continued down the deserted hall, the tiled floor changed to plush carpeting. He read the names on office doors until he found the one labeled Joel Frazier, CEO.

He decided against knocking. If his rudeness got Emma fired, too bad. He opened the door, scanning the illuminated office.

Two people occupied the office. Emma was bound hand and foot to a chair. A man, Frazier presumably, held a gun to her head. Her ghostly white face fueled his fear. Quentin swallowed the helpless rage billowing in his gut.

He had no weapon on him but that didn't matter. If it

weren't for the gun at Emma's head, he could take the smaller man easily. That gun changed everything.

Emma wasn't safe. He had to save her. If he failed—no, he couldn't think about that now. Her safety was his only priority. Bracing fear washed through his body. His arms and legs seemed to weigh a hundred pounds each. The slower he moved, the faster his thoughts raced.

That gun.

He had to neutralize the gun.

Get the gun.

Save the girl.

His gaze locked on the gun at her temple. "Emma?"

"You must be the boyfriend. Come in, Mr. Stone. We've been waiting for you."

"Who are you?" Quentin edged closer.

"Do as Joel says, Quentin." Emma's voice sounded dull.

"What do you want with us?" he asked.

"Isn't it obvious?" the gunman asked.

"The only thing that's obvious is the gun at Emma's head." Quentin pretended not to see the chair that Frazier indicated.

"That's because I intend to kill her." Frazier wiped the sweat from his brow with a trembling hand. "And you, too, of course, Mr. Stone. You have to die."

He searched for a makeshift weapon, but there wasn't even a magazine on Frazier's immaculate desk. "Why don't you put down the gun? We can work this out."

"Forget it. This gun is all that stands between me and hard time."

Quentin stopped about ten feet away. Growing up in construction had taught him a thing or two about fighting.

You used everything you had. His reach was longer. Thanks to his brothers, he had years of experience wrestling guys to the ground. If the gun were out of the picture, he could take the man. And he really wanted to pound Frazier for threatening to hurt Emma.

He couldn't let the man kill her. He couldn't bear to live without her.

He loved her.

He loved her. That protecting his heart stuff had been bull. He loved her, and he wouldn't let her down.

With that realization, he transformed from prey to predator. His primitive instincts roared to life. He had to save Emma.

The chill in his blood centered him. Too much heat and he wouldn't fight well. The icy clarity gave him the emotional distance he needed to assess the threat to his woman.

"What's this about, Frazier?" Quentin assumed a more balanced stance so he could spring forward at a moment's notice. "Is there a problem with her work performance?"

"I'm the best lab manager this place has ever had," Emma said. "Joel's snapped or something. Why did you come here? Why didn't you stay home where you'd be safe?"

He had to get the gun pointed toward him before he could make his move. His thoughts revved into overdrive searching for a strategy.

He remembered Frazier had once dated Emma. He thought of the words he would least like another man to say about Emma. "It's okay, sugar cakes. Your dream lover will take care of everything."

He prayed Emma didn't laugh aloud at his boasting.

Frazier should be furious at his sleeping with Emma. "What's the deal, Frazier? Are you upset because I've swept Emma off her feet and into *my* bed? Are you wondering how we spend our nights?"

The gun jerked, but the barrel remained at Emma's head. "Shut up. I don't believe you. Emma doesn't believe in casual sex."

"That may have been what she told you, but you don't have the equipment I've got." Quentin cupped himself crudely to accentuate his point. "She does whatever I tell her. She's submissive to my every desire."

He ignored her startled gasp and sensed the other man's resolve weakening. His chance to get the gun neared. "When we're not making love, we're talking about it. And when we're not talking about it, we're laughing at you."

"Liar," Joel snarled.

Frazier's full attention shifted to him, not on Emma. It was a matter of time before he trained the gun at Quentin. "You don't have what it takes, do you? You're not man enough for her. You're not man enough to fight me."

"Shut up! I'll swear you shot her and turned the gun on yourself."

Quentin inched closer. With his long legs, he could kick the gun out of the man's hand before he rushed him. "Why would I shoot her? I've got everything a man could need. A woman to cook and clean for me without the benefit of a marriage license. I can't lose. You have to come up with a better story than that, little man."

"I'm not short!" Frazier yelled.

He'd hit a nerve. He brought his fists up into a fighter's defensive position. "Yeah? You're *nothing*. My little brother could take you. You're not a man at all. You're a boy, trying to do a man's job."

Frazier aimed the gun at Quentin. As Frazier turned, Quentin lashed out with his foot.

The gun roared.

He registered Emma's bloodcurdling scream as his foot struck Frazier's gun hand. The weapon flipped end over end through the air. He plowed his fist into Joel Frazier's soft stomach. Frazier curled forward, raising his arms defensively, throwing wild punches. Quentin landed a flurry of punches on his face and trunk. The thud of flesh on flesh fueled his anger. This man intended to kill Emma.

His opponent's hands dropped. Quentin landed a strong right uppercut under his opponent's jaw. At that, Frazier's eyes rolled back in his head. He dropped to the floor, smacking his head against the desk.

Triumph roared through Quentin. He'd won. He'd beaten the man who wanted to kill Emma. He wiped the moisture from his face with the back of his hand, surprised at the blood he found.

He'd been shot?

He'd kicked the gun. He remembered that. Emma. He had to be strong for Emma.

His head hurt, but he felt strong otherwise. He wasn't ready to die. He fingered the area again, recoiling when he found a gash in his temple. It was true. He'd been shot.

How long did it take to die from a gunshot wound? How long did he have before he couldn't raise his fists? It didn't matter. He would fight as long as he was able. He'd do anything for Emma.

He was still alive, and Emma was safe.

"Night, night, loser," he said to Frazier.

"Quentin?" Emma's voice trembled. "Are you okay?"

He searched the floor for the gun. After he located it, he shoved it in his waistband. "Apparently it takes a lot to kill me." He turned to smile at Emma.

Her eyes widened at the sight of him, and she fainted. He caught her head as she slumped forward. Gently, he removed the ropes from her hands and feet and propped her in the chair.

He turned to Frazier, out cold on the floor. Bastard. He twisted the ropes tightly around Frazier's hands and feet. With the excess line, he bound the man's hands and feet together behind him and tossed him in the corner of the room. Good riddance.

He mopped his face with his hand again. More blood. Not good. He glanced down at his stained shirt. Ruined, but he had more. He tasted blood.

He needed to think. So much blood spilled. But he was still functioning. A flesh wound, perhaps. Those bled a lot.

No wonder Emma fainted.

He visualized the shooting trajectory from start to finish, turned and located the bullet in the wall. Relief swept through him. If the bullet was there, it wasn't in his head.

He took a few assessing breaths. He flexed his bruised fists. Frazier had never even landed a punch.

A wall of fatigue hit him. He needed to catch his breath. Carefully, he settled Emma in his lap, cradling her against his right side. Sleep beckoned, but he couldn't rest yet. He dialed the emergency number and summoned help.

His fingers stroked through Emma's auburn hair. He was never letting her out of his sight again. His heart couldn't take the strain. She could've been killed. The thought of losing her tore his heart in two.

Her eyelids fluttered. "Quentin?"

She was coming around. Good. He inhaled her soothing scent. God, he was tired. He didn't remember ever being so tired.

He kissed her eyes closed. "Red, don't be alarmed. There's a little blood on my shirt."

Her eyes opened wide. "You crazy man. Do you think you're bullet proof? Why did you step in front of a bullet?"

"For you," he whispered. "I did it for you."

The room shifted and grew black.

* * *

Emma shrieked as he collapsed beneath her. She scrambled off his lap, her heart racing. There was so much blood. On him. On her.

Was he dead?

Had his last moment on earth been spent with her yelling at him? With trembling hands, she checked his pulse and found a faint beat. She closed her eyes in relief.

She drew in a ragged breath, forcing herself to think. She had to help him. The wound. Where was it? Why couldn't she remember?

Everything happened so fast.

Quentin had taunted Joel. The gun fired. That's all she remembered.

She gripped her hands tightly together. The man she loved had gone up against an armed man. For her.

Quentin didn't have to prove anything to her. She knew he was hero material, but he wasn't bulletproof. She drew in another ragged breath. He'd nearly died for her. She had to hold it together. She couldn't fail him now.

On rubbery legs, Emma walked back to Joel's desk and dialed the phone. The emergency operator informed her that the police were on their way. She requested an ambulance and terminated the call.

She saw red.

Everywhere.

She had to stop the bleeding.

Think, Emma.

Gravity would cause the blood to flow toward the ground, so she searched for the wound on Quentin's head. She blotted his forehead with tissues from Joel's desk. The tissues turned bright red. A sob ripped from her throat. She grabbed another hunk of tissues. They turned to a sodden mess immediately. Not good enough. She needed something more substantial.

What?

What could she use to staunch the blood flow?

Her gaze flitted around the office. There. On the door. Joel's pristine lab coat. She grabbed it and pressed it against the oozing wound.

Quentin couldn't die.

She needed him.

Where was that ambulance?

What was taking them so long?

The hospital wasn't far from Orbital, five minutes max.

Where were they?

She lifted the coat and stared at the wound. Blood

welled up and trickled down his face. Emma released the breath she'd been holding and forced herself to take another breath. She applied steady pressure to the wound. Quentin couldn't bleed to death. Not after he'd saved her life.

"You ruined everything, Emma."

She jumped at the sound of Joel's angry voice. She'd forgotten about him. Where was he? Where was the gun?

She glanced around the room. There he was. Tossed in the corner. Bound hand and foot on the floor. Hogtied, like the pig he was.

Quentin must have done that before he'd passed out. She smiled grimly. "Doesn't feel so good to be tied up does it?"

"Bitch." Joel struggled against his bonds. "Untie me right now."

Words boiled out of her mouth. "Forget it. You tried to kill me. Why? Is it because I wouldn't go out with you?"

Joel snorted. "You wrecked my marketing scheme."

Her gaze narrowed. "What marketing scheme? The business dinners?"

His harsh laughter grated on her ears. "You were so passionate, so sincere about Orbital that every one of those chumps handed me a fist-full of money. I got the cash, and you got the shaft. Stupid girl."

"Did you do those other things to me? Did you saw the joists in my house?"

"Yeah, I cut your floor. I figured if you couldn't live in that dump you'd move back into town. I didn't like having to go so far to check up on you."

"You're a worm. I can't believe how despicable you are. I can't believe you checked up on me, ever. What about my tires? You cut them, too?"

"Why would I cut your tires? I wanted you to come to me. Someone else did that. Let me go, and I'll kill them for you."

Emma yelled her frustration. She nudged Joel hard with her foot. "Think again, moron. You're headed to prison."

CHAPTER SIXTEEN

Quentin's family swirled around Emma in the Emergency Room lobby. She needed to see him, to touch him, to know he was still alive. Instead, she sat here and waited for the police and doctors to finish up.

She saw red, only this time the red dotted her hands, her clothes, her hair. Quentin's blood. Please, God, don't let him die, she prayed silently. I love him so. Even if he thinks he's faster than a speeding bullet. She offered God everything and anything if he would spare Quentin.

She couldn't stop shaking. She clutched her hands together in her lap. What was taking so long?

Dottie covered Emma's trembling bloodstained hands with hers. "Dear, it's going to be all right. God wouldn't take Quentin. Not when he's finally happy."

Tears welled in her eyes. "I should have quit that job long ago. I'm sorry. I never should have put him in danger. If he hadn't met me, he wouldn't be in the hospital."

Lucy touched Emma's shoulder. "You can't blame

yourself. And you two would have met. I planned to introduce you, remember?"

Didn't they see she was responsible for his injury? "He loves my house. If he hadn't seen the house, maybe he wouldn't have liked me."

Jeanie choked out a laugh. "You're funny. Quentin likes you so much it's almost painful for us to watch him when he's with you. There's no way he likes your house more than you."

Alf draped his black leather jacket around her trembling shoulders. He sat beside her. "Face facts. Quentin loves you."

She sprang to her feet and paced the room. She couldn't accept their comfort. Not when this was her fault.

She loved Quentin so much it hurt. Why had he taken on an armed man? Didn't he care about his safety? She couldn't allow him to be so reckless with his precious skin.

She shivered again, remembering the chill of the gun barrel pressed to her temple. She could go the rest of her life without ever seeing another pistol. Quentin had responsibilities. A company to run. A family that depended on him for their livelihood. A woman that loved him with every molecule of her being. He had no right to take chances with his life.

A medical professional wearing floral patterned scrubs and a stethoscope draped around her neck approached the family.

John rose. "Well?"

"Mr. Stone will be fine," the nurse said. "Once the police finish questioning him, two family members may see him."

Emma halted. Quentin was all right. Relief trickled through her body, warming her. He would be okay.

"What about the wound?" Lucy asked. "Did you find the bullet? Will he have any side effects?"

The nurse frowned. "Mr. Stone's scalp wound isn't life threatening. We're replacing the fluid he lost while we prepare to stitch his face." She pursed her lips. "He could've waited for a plastic surgeon to do the stitches, but he said he didn't mind having a scar. He's a lucky man. If the bullet trajectory had varied, the result would've been fatal."

Emma's calm evaporated. Her nerves couldn't take this yo-yoing from one emotional extreme to another. She ran straight for Quentin's cubicle.

"Miss. Stop. You can't go in there."

She ignored the nurse's command. She had to see Quentin right now. Throwing aside the curtain, she stepped into the area. Two cops filled one side of the cubicle, two nurses stood on his other side. A gel pack lay across Quentin's forehead. His dark brown eyes lit up at the sight of her.

She stopped at the foot of the gurney. "You could have been killed. Didn't you think about your responsibilities before you stepped in front of that bullet?"

Monitors pinged in the abrupt silence. The glare from all the shiny chrome in the room blinded her. Tears poured down Emma's cheeks. In the sudden absence of sight, her pulse thundered through her ears.

"Whose jacket are you wearing?" Quentin's voice sliced through the air.

John hooked his arm around her shoulders. "Don't yell at sweet Emma. She's had a rough day."

"And I haven't?" Quentin asked.

"This is highly irregular," snapped a nurse. "You cannot be in here. Please leave."

"Come here, Emma," Quentin said.

She couldn't move. "I don't like being bossed around. When will you get that through that thick head of yours?"

Lucy's arm snugged around Emma's waist. "His head is pretty thick all right. Thick enough to repel a bullet."

His family sandwiched her. This time she didn't feel crowded. This time she needed their support because something was wrong with her knees. If anyone moved, she would fall flat on her face.

"Marry me."

His demand filtered through the chaos in her head. Her heart raced. Time suspended. There was no past, no future, only this moment.

Marry him?

Not a chance in the world.

She loved him too much to risk an engagement.

Marriage would ruin everything. Besides, he hadn't asked her to marry him, he'd ordered her to marry him. "I won't do it. I won't become another ex-fiancée. I love you too much for that."

"Who said anything about an engagement?" he growled. "We're getting married without an engagement."

She exhaled slowly.

He was okay.

If she kept saying it, pretty soon she might believe it. "We can't. There are a million reasons why we can't get married right away. The first is that your sister is getting married this Saturday. You can't ruin her big day."

"Jeanie!" Quentin bellowed. "Get in here."

Jeanie took Lucy's place at her side. "Quit yelling at her," Jeanie ordered. "What do you want with me?"

"Emma won't marry me because you're getting married," Quentin complained.

Jeanie laughed. "I'm not postponing my wedding. Harrison and Mom would kill me."

"I'm not asking you to change the date. I'm asking you if you mind if I get married in the next few days. Will that take away from your big day?"

"No. You can get married anytime you like. In fact, now that I think about it, sooner is better for your wedding date. Your fiancées have a habit of getting away from you."

"Well, Emma?"

The policemen and the nurses seemed riveted by the conversation. Emma desired privacy, but it was a luxury she didn't have. Quentin seemed set on the idea of marrying her. "No. The answer is no. I can't afford a wedding. I'm in the middle of a rehab. And I don't have a wedding dress."

"I'll take care of everything," Quentin promised. "Say you'll marry me."

Fear clutched her heart. Agreeing to marry him would make her his fiancée. She had to be strong for both of them. "Why can't we go on as before? Why do we have to get married?"

He groaned. "You're killing me. I'm a red-blooded American male. I want you to be my wife in every sense of the word."

Her temperature rose. She fanned the heat away from her face. "You're embarrassing me."

"I'm a desperate man, Red."

Dottie moved John aside and took his place supporting her. "I see that the marriage negotiations have stalled. Emma, do you love my son?"

"Yes," Emma whispered, her eyes never leaving Quentin's face.

"My son is a handsome man, he's a great provider, and he's true blue. You won't get a better offer. What's the problem here?"

Emma couldn't take her gaze off Quentin's beloved face. Liquid heat curled through her body, scorching her thoughts. What was the problem? Oh yeah, she remembered.

Marriage.

A bad idea.

"Quentin hasn't told me that he loves me," she said. "I won't marry a man who is afraid to face his feelings. My father deserted my family when he couldn't face his feelings. I learned from that mistake. No matter how much I love Quentin, I'm not entering into a one-sided relationship."

"Who says it's one-sided?" Quentin rumbled. He sat up. "I love you, Emma. I've loved you from the first minute I saw you painting that barn. I can't think what my life would be like without you in it. I love everything about you, from the way your red hair curls to the way you go toe-to-toe with me over every detail. I love you with all my heart, and I want the world to know."

Emma couldn't breathe.

Quentin loved her.

"She's crying again," Alf said.

"Say you'll marry me. Please?"

Her heart overflowed with love. He loved her. She

was sure of him in a way she'd never been sure of any other man. His character was strong where her father's had been weak. Anyone who held his family together like Quentin had done wouldn't run in the face of adversity. Anyone who'd take a bullet for her wouldn't abandon her.

"Yes. I'll marry you," she whispered.

A wild cheer errupted in the Emergency Room. She glanced around in surprise. Doctors, nurses, and police officers grinned at her. Stones and Sterlings, too. Her face flushed with heat. How many people had witnessed the proposal?

Quentin lay back down, his eyes glinting in satisfaction. "Lady, you are a piece of work. I never thought I'd have to haggle with a woman to get her to marry me."

Dottie beamed. "I have the perfect thought. Why not make it a double wedding? I'm sure Jeanie and Harrison won't mind."

Jeanie reappeared at Emma's side and kissed Emma's cheek. "I'd be honored."

A double wedding?

Emma's mind reeled.

She was getting married.

On Saturday. To the handsomest man on the earth. "How can it happen so fast? Aren't there licenses and blood tests?"

"This is Maryland. You don't need a blood test. You've got a valid photo ID, cash, and forty-eight hours until your wedding date, right?" Jeanie asked.

Emma nodded.

"That's all you need to get your marriage license. Hey, look at it this way, you won't have the hassle of selecting the location, the caterer, the photographer, the musicians, the reception site, the party favors. It's all done."

The walls of the curtained room closed in on Emma. In the span of a few hours, she had been held at gunpoint, agonized over Quentin's gunshot wound, and accepted a wedding proposal.

Now she was supposed to get married this weekend?

CHAPTER SEVENTEEN

"What do you think of this one?"

The white gown Beverly held up looked expensive. Emma frowned. "How much is it?"

"Don't focus on price yet," her sister said. "Let's figure out what styles work and then we can do cost comparisons."

Maddy waved to Emma from a fitting room. "I've made my selections. Come on in, Emma."

She was getting married on Saturday. The notion had seemed surreal until she was confronted with dozens of white gowns. Her feet stuck to the plush carpet. "This is ridiculous. I can't get married. I'm making a big mistake."

Maddy firmly gripped her arm. She propelled her towards the fitting room. "You're not making a mistake. You're getting married so that Beverly and I can get married."

She jolted forward at Maddy's ridiculous statement. "What?"

"We're counting on you to break the curse, so to speak." Beverly scooted around her to hang up another gown on the hook. "You've got a dreamboat of a man who worships the ground you walk on. We figure if you can make it work with him, both of us might have a shot at marriage."

With a flip of her wrist, Maddy snapped the curtain shut. She unzipped Emma's sundress. "You're the guinea pig in the science project of our lives."

Memories of the previous day raced into her thoughts. The horror of being held at gunpoint would never fade. Or worse, the sight of Quentin's blood everywhere. She shivered. "I can't think about science right now. Science reminds me of Orbital and Joel. I can't believe I ever dated that creep."

Maddy unzipped a gown. She motioned Emma into it. "I can't believe Joel blamed you for his fraudulent investment scheme going down the drain," Maddy said. "Did you have any idea he pocketed that investment money?"

Emma wiggled. The strapless lace gown sagged open, revealing a large amount of bare bosom. Unacceptable. She took it off. "I had no idea it was a scam. All those people lost their money because of me. I feel awful. How could I have been so naïve?"

"Don't let Joel bring you down to his level. Your passion for your work persuaded those people to invest. That's a rare gift," Beverly countered loyally.

"Besides, your intuition told you something was wrong with Joel because you never slept with him," Maddy said. "Deep down you knew he was wrong for you."

"Thanks for the vote of confidence." Emma stepped

into another gown. "It felt wrong with him from the beginning, but I assumed it was my fault. The odd part is I really wanted it to work with him. On the surface, he was a successful executive. I wanted to marry and raise a family. But not with creepy Joel. Thank God, I didn't let him seduce me."

"Did your life flash before your eyes?" Maddy peered over her shoulder to view the sleek satin gown in the full-length mirror. Emma unzipped the clingy gown without comment and selected another one from the group. "What was it like to have a gun pointed at your head?"

Emma swallowed thickly. "Scary. And then I got mad. I didn't want to be a victim. I wanted to be home with Quentin. Which scared me all over because I knew Quentin would come looking for me at work, and he wouldn't stop looking until he found me. I was terrified Joel would shoot Quentin the minute he walked through the door."

"But it turned out great. Quentin disarmed Joel, and he proposed to you." Beverly sighed dreamily. "It's so romantic."

"You left out the part about the weapon firing. That wasn't romantic at all. And it wasn't romantic watching Quentin bleed all over everything. I couldn't tell if the bullet had gone into his head or not. He was out cold. I've never seen so much blood."

Maddy plucked at the puffy sleeves of the wedding gown Emma wore. "Enough about the blood already. I don't want to hear the gory details."

"This gown isn't bad. Let's put it in a maybe pile," Beverly suggested. "How will the people get their money back if Joel spent it?"

Emma stared at her reflection in the mirror. Did she like this dress? She didn't feel strongly one way or the other. "I'm not sure. All I know is I'm not liable for it. Joel's aunt got a list of names from me last night at the police station. She'll contact the investors to work something out."

"Joel was behind everything that happened to you?" Maddy asked.

Emma shook her head. "Actually, no. The police arrested one of Quentin's ex-fiancées, a woman named Janice Green, for slashing my tires. She wanted me out of his life."

"Was she stalking you? Will you have to look over your shoulder for the rest of your life?" Maddy asked.

"We won't have any more trouble from Janice. She wrote out a check for the full price of the tires and apologized to both of us. Now that she knows he isn't available, she's changed her tune."

"You've certainly had a time of it this month," Beverly observed wryly. "Is there anyone else lurking out there on the horizon we need to worry about?"

Who knew she had all these enemies? "I was concerned about a coworker, Herb Goodlow. But his bad mood stemmed from his frustration as an unpublished writer. Lucy found his manuscript when she hacked into Herb's work computer. He's harmless."

"You're quitting your job at Orbital?" Beverly asked.

"Yes. There's a lot to do to the Heartly Inn before the grand opening. I'm thinking about reupholstering the living room pieces. I need to join a B&B Association and finalize my marketing plan."

"I'll help with fabric selection and color schemes," Maddy volunteered.

Emma blinked back tears. "Thanks, but I'm on a budget. I can't afford you or your pricey fabrics. Besides, I want the Heartly Inn to be comfortable. I don't want a swanky downtown hotel look."

Maddy sniffed. "I'd like to help. You've done so much for me, it's the least I can do to get you started. I'll donate the cost of the materials and my labor if you'll let me do the living room."

"I'd like to help, too," Beverly added with teary eyes.

Great. She'd made everyone cry. "Thanks. I appreciate your help."

Maddy fluffed out the skirt of the next gown. "This is so exciting. You're getting married."

Exciting? Not quite.

Terrifying. Thrilling. Painful. Wonderful. But not exciting...yet.

"Lately my life has been a speeding freight train." Emma preened in the ballroom-style gown. "This one reminds me of Cinderella. Do you think we could get a pumpkin coach on short notice?"

Beverly cleared her throat delicately. "You're not, you know? I mean, you don't *have* to get married, do you?"

"Not a chance." Emma's eyes twinkled back at her in the mirror. "Quentin can't hold onto his fiancées, so he insisted our engagement be short. That's the reason for the rush."

"How many times has he been engaged?" Beverly asked.

She shrugged. "It doesn't matter to me. The point is the man has good reason to be scared of long engagements."

"I don't blame you for jumping in with both feet," Maddy said. "Quentin is the best looking man I've ever met in my life. I'd marry him in a red-hot minute."

A searing flash of jealousy heated her blood. "Quentin's mine. He loves me. He's marrying *me*."

"See? I knew this marriage wasn't a mistake." Maddy nodded to Beverly to hand her the next gown. "You have very strong feelings for the man. He's your passion."

"Yeah." Emma sighed. "But what's to keep him from walking out when we have three kids? Better yet, what's to keep me from turning into Mom?"

"That's nerves talking. You're not Mom," Beverly jiggled the zipper until it closed fully. "With your college degree, you've got wage-earning potential and you'll have the Heartly Inn. No way you'll turn into Mom. We won't allow it. Neither will Quentin."

Emma stared blankly into the mirror. If she had to wear this gown, the wedding was off. "I hate this gown. I look like a plumped up marshmallow on a stick."

Beverly slid the gown off. She handed it to Maddy. "No one said every gown would work. That's why you're trying them on. We only need to find one that suits you."

Emma sighed and stepped into another gown. "It doesn't seem possible. How can I be a Heartly and be happy or married?"

Maddy laughed. "You won't be a Heartly. You'll be a Stone. Unless you're planning on having one of those hyphenated double last names."

"This gown makes me look like one of those stacked washer-dryer combinations." The ivory column gown Emma had on did not tuck in at her waist. "Of course I plan to change my name. I wouldn't dream of not taking his name. Quentin and I are both traditional about that sort of thing."

Beverly reached for the single gown she'd selected. "Being traditional is not bad. It gives you a solid framework. Something most Heartlys have never had."

"What if it doesn't work out? How will I pick up the pieces of my broken heart? I was shattered when my relationship with Joel ended. In retrospect, I didn't love him. If it doesn't work out with Quentin, I won't be able to function."

Beverly smoothed the chiffon overskirt of the A-line gown. "There are no guarantees in life, Em. Love is what we all seek. It makes life worth living. It's why people take a chance on marriage."

Emma closed her gaping mouth. "Is that your professional opinion or sisterly wisdom?"

"Does it matter? I want you to be happy."

"Me, too," echoed Maddy.

Emma stared at the three expectant faces in the full-length mirror. Her sisters wanted her to be happy. Gradually she noticed the gown she wore. It tucked in just so at her waist.

She turned side to side to assess the different aspects of the dress. The smile on her face stretched from ear to ear. "Ladies. We have a winner."

"And the winner is you, Emma Heartly," Beverly said as she and Maddy swallowed Emma in a group hug.

After a moment, Emma collected herself. "Okay. Now we need to find two fairly similar bridesmaid dresses in stock."

"I saw some really cute black dresses on the rack out there," Maddy added hopefully.

She eyed the black silk sheath Maddy wore. "Forget

it, Sis. No black dresses at my wedding."

"They wouldn't have those dresses here if they weren't appropriate for weddings," Maddy protested.

"Too bad. My two bridesmaids will wear happy colors."

"The old Emma is back." Maddy winked at Beverly.

"Yep. She's bossing us around again," Maddy said.

Emma retorted, "It's for your own good."

"You don't know how much we hate those words."

She remembered being on the losing ends of debates with Quentin. "Believe me, I feel your pain. Quentin says those words to me all the time."

* * *

Emma's heart sang with joy as Quentin's lips covered hers. The sounds of the wedding reception faded from the gazebo. This man was her husband. For better or for worse. He'd promised he'd be there for her, no matter what.

Their tongues parried, hinting at the intimacy to come that night. She'd waited thirty years to experience passion with her husband. The moment had arrived.

Her hands fisted in the lapels of his tux. His fingers spanned her waist and inched higher, eliciting waves of wonderful anticipation.

If they weren't at the wedding reception, she'd be removing his clothes. She whimpered in frustration. He smelled great, felt even better.

He was her *husband*.

Delicious thoughts flitted through her head. She'd be living her dream at last.

Quentin was the real deal, the man of her dreams, the

man who would share her life. The man she loved wholeheartedly.

She thrilled to his touch, wishing for privacy. She blushed from head to toe, thinking of intimacy, but Quentin's love gave her courage.

As the kiss ended, she clung to his strength, his rock solidness. The sensations he stirred up energized her. She'd never felt so alive with any other man.

"Thinking about tonight?" he asked.

She drew a feather light circle around the arc of small black stitches on his brow. The bright gold band on her left hand glistened in the late afternoon sunlight. "I was thinking how nontraditional our wedding pictures will be with these stitches on your forehead. You're going to have a scar on your face."

He held her at arm's length. "Does that matter to you?"

Emma chuckled. "Heck, no. I figure every time you see that mark you'll think of me. Your scar-to-be is marriage insurance."

His arms relaxed, drawing her close. He nuzzled her neck. "I like the idea of a scar. This old mug should look like I feel, and I aged twenty years after seeing that gun pointed at your head. I'll never forget that."

Her arms tightened around his waist. "You're my hero. I never thought I needed anyone. I was wrong. I'll always need you."

His hands cradled her face, lifting it up for a very proprietary kiss. Pure lightning sluiced though her veins, filling her head with erotic notions.

"All right, you two. There'll be time enough for that later." Lucy mounted the gazebo steps to join them. "What's this I hear about a two-week-long honeymoon? I need Emma at Orbital, Quentin. You can't have her that long."

With reluctance, Emma stepped away from her husband. He snagged her hand. The contact buzzed through her, adding to the anticipation pulsing through her veins. Her fingers curled around his.

"Too bad," he said. "After what we've been through, we deserve at least two weeks away from the pressures of daily life."

Lucy winked suggestively. "Not to mention the personal recreation involved in a honeymoon."

A dangerous smile flitted across Quentin's face. "You can't have her, Luce. This is my honeymoon. I'm not cutting it short for any reason."

"But Emma knows everything about Orbital. She can have the whole place reorganized in a few days. I'll limp along until y'all get back."

"Congratulations on your promotion to CEO, Lucy," Emma stepped forward to kiss her friend's cheek. "But don't count on me coming back to Orbital. Now that Heartly Inn is nearing completion, I'm devoting myself to launching the Inn. I need to get a website up and get myself linked to the right associations, and there's my marketing plan to finish. I'll be busy pulling everything together."

"I've considered that. I'm willing to have you work part-time for Orbital so you'll also have time for the Inn. Once I explained my dilemma to the family, they agreed to help pitch in with the Inn when I need you at Orbital. You need to make your recipes available to us so we'll know what to prepare."

"Uh, well," Emma hemmed. "I haven't been successful with the cooking end of things yet, but I have high hopes that I'm close."

Quentin's hand twitched in hers. She glanced up at the laughter dancing in his eyes. Drat. With the shooting and the wedding preparations, she hadn't asked Quentin to be her resident chef. It was the logical solution to her dilemma.

"You could always hire someone to cook for you," Lucy suggested helpfully.

Why would she do that when she lived with a gourmet cook? The question burned in her throat, but she held it in. This was Quentin's secret. If he didn't want his family to know about it, she respected his wishes.

"I'm going to be Emma's breakfast chef," Quentin said.

"You are?" His outburst stunned her. Why would he reveal his secret now? What had changed? She watched him for a cue.

"Yeah. I'm a good cook."

He seemed relaxed, not edgy like she would have expected for the big revelation. Whatever was going on, he wanted this out in the open. Not a problem. She believed in him one hundred percent.

"The best," Emma added with a nod. "Quentin makes every dish special. With him in the kitchen, Heartly Inn will win all kinds of awards for culinary excellence."

"Wait a minute. *Quentin* is a good cook?" Lucy fixed her brother with a piercing look. "Are you telling me that you're the secret restaurant that made all those fabulous desserts?" Lucy's shoulders shook until she doubled over with laughter.

Emma's fingers tightened around Quentin's. Lucy was a friend, but Quentin came first in Emma's pecking order. She frowned at her friend. "Yes, he is."

"Well, hot damn." Lucy wiped the tears from her eyes. "We've got a chef in the family."

His family crowded into the small gazebo. "What's this? Quentin cooks?" John asked.

"I do." Quentin moved closer to his brother, his deep voice carrying across the wedding grounds. All heads turned toward the gazebo. "You have a problem with that?"

She stepped between them. "Because if you do, I'll make sure you never eat another bite of his cooking again."

"Easy, Red." Quentin's voice softened. "John doesn't know how to handle temperamental females."

"You two deserve each other," John said. "Why the big secret, bro?"

Once again, the answer burned in Emma's throat. She wanted to fight this battle for him, but she couldn't. He had to wrestle with his own demons. It was up to him how much he told his family.

Quentin shrugged. "I've always liked fooling around in the kitchen. I wasn't sure what the family would think, so I kept it to myself."

"We'd be crazy to say anything bad about your cooking, especially now that you've got big bad Emma to protect you," John teased.

"I love your cooking," Jeanie volunteered. "I don't suppose you'd consider teaching Harrison how to cook."

"Don't even think about it, Jeanie," Harrison warned. "I've got my hands full with too many other things. But I'll sample Quentin's cooking anytime he needs a taster."

Lucy shook her head in wonder. "I can't believe you felt you had to hide part of yourself from us. I've got to tell Mom."

"Let me. It's my wedding day," Jeanie said. She gathered up her gown and raced down the steps with Lucy and Harrison at her heels.

Emma breathed a sigh of relief at their departure. That had gone amazingly well. Even better, Quentin didn't seem out of sorts after his secret came out. She longed to ask him what had changed, but she had the rest of their lives to do that.

Quentin turned to his brother. "Everything all set out at the Inn?"

"While you're on your honeymoon, I'll stay there on the weekdays," John said. "Maddy will cover the weekends."

At the mention of her sister's name, Emma scanned the crowd of wedding guests for her family. Beverly was chatting with an older couple by the buffet; Maddy was talking to Quentin's younger brother near the bar. She filled with pride at the strong women they'd become.

"Why don't you give Alf more responsibility while I'm away?" Quentin asked. "He's ready. I'm thinking to explore this cooking thing at the Heartly Inn. Maybe even do a full scale restaurant out there."

Emma blinked. "A restaurant?"

"What?" John scowled. "Who will run the company? Who will do our estimating and rehab jobs?"

"Think about a three-way split while I'm gone. I want less corporate responsibility. You've done a great job with the new starts. Alf has learned enough about the technical aspects of construction to move up into management."

Emma couldn't believe what she was hearing. Was Quentin walking away from his family's business? Was he serious about cooking at the inn? When was he going to discuss this with her?

John looked dazed. "I want to make sure I heard you correctly. You want Alf to do your job while you're gone?"

"Yes."

With that, Quentin shepherded her down the gazebo steps and around the house. She followed his lead, hoping for privacy to hash over the sweeping statements he'd made. First Quentin revealed his secret, now he was leaving the family firm?

"Quentin?" she asked.

John trailed them. "Where are you going? You didn't cut your wedding cake yet. Mom will be upset if you leave early."

"Mom will understand. So will everyone else. Have fun. Don't think about work anymore today. I know I won't."

"I'll see you in two weeks then." John nodded and turned on his heel.

"We're leaving?" Emma's heart raced in her chest. "What about all those things you said?"

"I meant every word of them. I plan to enjoy our honeymoon." A sexy grin lit his face. "As of right now, we're officially underway."

"But your family? Your job? I don't understand."

He smoothed his hand down her cheek, eliciting an exciting shiver. "They'll be here when I get back. I'm making workload adjustments now that I've got a family, that's all."

"And your secret?"

"Is a secret no more."

"You're okay with that?"

"I'm more than okay with it. You gave me the courage to face that fear." His eyebrows waggled seductively. "I'm ready to give you your reward."

Heat flashed through her. She caught up the hem of her gown. "Race you to the car?"

"I've got an even better idea." He scooped her into his arms and jogged the remaining distance. "I've wanted to do this since the first moment I saw you. What would you have said if I'd carried you off in my Jeep that first day?"

"I'd have opened the car door for you."

"Are you happy?"

Emma beamed. "I wouldn't change a thing."

Inside the Jeep, Quentin paused. "Does our courtship meet the standards of your romance novels?"

He'd swept her off her feet from day one. He was her hero in so many ways, she couldn't name them all. But no point in giving the man a big head. She had to live with him for the rest of her life.

"We hit all the highlights of both our favorite kinds of books," she said. "Action and adventure for you, and a handsome hero rescuing a woman in jeopardy for me."

"You forgot about the happily-ever-after part." He sped down the road.

"No chance of forgetting that." She beamed. "It's my new reality."

"I'll still be bossy," Quentin warned.

"Me, too. What's a little bossiness amongst friends?"

"We're more than friends. You love me."

Emma chucked him lightly under the chin. "Yes, I do. And it's a good thing since you're so bossy."

"Look who's talking."

ABOUT THE AUTHOR

A scientist by training, a romanticist at heart, award-winning author Maggie Toussaint loves to solve puzzles. Whether it's the puzzle of a relationship or a who-dun-it, she tackles them all with equal aplomb and wonder. Maggie writes cozy mystery and romantic suspense books. Her first novel won Best Romantic Suspense in the 2007 National Readers Choice Awards. Her previous titles include HOUSE OF LIES, NO SECOND CHANCE, MUDDY WATERS, and IN FOR A PENNY. Her upcoming mystery releases include ON THE NICKEL (March 2011), book two of the Cleopatra Jones cozy mystery series and DEATH, ISLAND STYLE (February 2012). She freelances for a weekly newspaper. Visit her at www.maggietoussaint.com and http://mudpiesandmagnolias.blog